ALEX: A WINGS OF DIABLO PREQUEL

WINGS OF DIABLO MC

RAE B. LAKE

ACKNOWLEDGMENTS

To my leader- I know there are times you don't know if your decisions are the right ones but I'll just say, right or wrong I'm going to be by your side!

To my little wings- You girls are growing so big. I hope you will always try to do what's right even when no one else does.

To my Friends, Family and Readers - Thank you so much for sticking through my journey. For all those that wanted to know how my WOD boys started out here's a quick taste!

SPECIAL MENTION!

Tina W. G.- Girl, this novella is especially for you. You have been riding with me since the very beginning and I can't even begin to tell you how grateful I am for all your kind words and encouragement. Not to mention your kick-ass comments! Thank you!

AUTHORS NOTE

Hey to all my Family, Friends, and Readers!

This novella is a long time coming! I just want to let all those who have read my Wings of Diablo series that this story takes place years before Wire, which is the first full-length book in the series.

Alex is such an important character to me and writing this story truly had me in my feels.

I hope you enjoy reading this story as much as I enjoyed writing it!

DISCLAIMER

This book includes several graphic traumatic events that may be troubling/triggering for some readers. Discretion is advised.

CHAPTER

Alex

"That's absolutely ridiculous. You've been smoking too much weed, that shit is really fucking you up." Gin scoffs, and we walk behind Clean as he takes us on a fucking journey to the backside of the property. We've been here a few years already, but with all the surrounding conflict, Prime has barely had a chance to make any modifications to the surrounding land. Archer joined us from the service, and he's been itching to get a better perimeter set up. The man is absolutely anal about our safety. He's going to be good for us, I can tell.

"Alex, you believe me, right?" Clean looks over at me and I simply shrug. I don't understand why anyone would be dumb enough to plant something in their enemy's backyard. Why the fuck would anyone want to do that?

"You guys have no faith." Clean huffs out and continues to storm in that direction.

"Of course, we don't have any faith, you spend all

your time trying to find a club bunny to fall into or a fucking pizza to shove in your mouth." Gin bites out.

"I gotta eat and I gotta fuck." He shrugs one shoulder and I can't help but laugh. I wish we could all have his carefree attitude.

After walking a bit further, he finally stops and points to a spot near a patch of brush. It's over runned with weeds and full of debris.

"Clean, there's nothing there." Gin throws his hands up and tries to walk away.

"For fucks sake, just help me for five minutes, if there's nothing here you can go about your boring lives. But if you want to get a little filthy with me...?" Clean's voice trails off, and he waggles his eyebrows. Which only cause me and Gin to groan in annoyance.

"Shut up, where did you see it?" I ask. Early this morning, Clean told us that he'd been taking a piss out of his window of all places, and he saw some random person digging in our backyard. By the time he got downstairs, the mystery man was gone.

The three of us start digging in the area where Clean saw the trespasser rooting around.

"Holy fuck, you can't be serious." Gin calls out while he pushes away some dirt, and we see a large brown package.

Someone really came into our territory and made it a drop-off. This is fucking crazy. I stand and wipe my hands off on my pants. When I came out here I thought we'd find some stupid box with a dead cat in it or something, but from the look of this package, it's no household pet. That only means Prime is going to be pissed off.

"WHAT THE FUCK do you mean someone stashed two kilos of coke in our backyard? Who? Why the fuck wasn't we all called to action when it was fucking happening?" Prime roars and we all flinch. The man is in his late forties, but he's still as brutal as he ever was.

"My bad Prime, I didn't know what I was seeing until it was almost over. I was drunk out of my mind." Clean offers.

"Of course you were. You're always fucking out of your mind, Barry! Fuck." Prime runs a hand over his face. "Who do we think did it?"

Prime looks over to me and then to Max, our Sergeant at Arms.

"I have several guesses, but if we step to any of them it means a nasty fight." Max responds.

"We just fucking got a bit of peace. We've barely got to a place where I don't have to call lockdowns every five seconds. What the fuck!" Prime roars again. Ever since his granddaughter was born Prime has been trying to get the club out of trouble and on good terms with all the surrounding MC's unfortunately that dream has yet to come to fruition.

"Okay, fine, we have to be very careful about what we do. I don't want this blowing up, and we start a war with the wrong fucking club.

"Either way, we're going to war. "

"No shit, I just need to make sure that we're going to war with the right crew. What the fuck is the point of getting on good terms with a crew If we're only going to accuse them of doing some shady shit in the next breath." Prime says.

I scoff and look away, but I don't say a word.

"You have something different to say Alex? Please open your fucking mouth and tell us all." Prime crosses his arms over his chest and glares at me.

I respect Prime, and I understand he's all about the brotherhood and our way of life but part of me feels like all this talk about trying to maintain peace makes us look weaker. I'd never fucking tell him that, though. I'm not an idiot.

"Prime, I'm with whatever plan you got but it seems like whoever thought it was a good idea to dump that shit here wasn't really concerned about playing nice with us." I keep his gaze for a second before I look away. I don't want him to think I'm trying to go against his word. As the President, if Prime told us to run around with our dicks swinging in the wind we'd have to do it because his word is law.

"We'll play it safe for now, but once we find out who this is, then we'll show them how much of a fucking mistake they made underestimating us." Prime nods once, and he turns to walk back to the clubhouse.

As I watch him walk away for the first time, instead of the strong proud man I've grown to respect as a mentor and a leader I see a tired man. He's been fighting a long time and from the looks of things, it seems like the fighting is far from over.

CHAPTER 2

Alex

THE POUNDING BASS OF THE MUSIC BLARING FROM THE speakers around the clubhouse makes me grind my teeth harder. I'm sitting at the in-house bar trying to dull my anger, but it's not helping. It's been a week, and we still have no idea who left the fucking coke back there. We all have our suspicions, but it's Gin who is our information manager, he's the one that's supposed to find this shit out.

I'm tired of fucking waiting. Shit needs to be handled now.

I grab my glass, but before I can pull it up to my lips a pair of arthritic hands pulls it away, "Boy, all these fucking women in here shaking their ass and tits and you sitting in front of me looking like your dog just fucking died." Mick leans down, so he can yell in my ear over the music. I'd mush his face away if he was one of the original members, even though he can't ride anymore we all respect him as an OG. I wince in pain but let him continue to yell in my ear. "You keep this shit up, you're going to end up driving yourself crazy, Alex. What's meant to fucking happen will happen." He pulls back and puts a small glass in front of me on the bar. He pours me about two knuckles worth of Jack Daniel's and moves down the bar to get someone else's order. He may not be able to ride with us, but he's a wing for life.

I slam my glass down on the bar and turn around on the stool I'm sitting on. Mick is right, the club bunnies are in rare form tonight. It's probably because we just took on three new ones. The more known we get as a crew the more the bunnies want to be a part of our life. Most of them don't stay, the only one that has been with us for longer than a year now is everyone's favorite long-haired prima ballerina, Cherry. She's really taken to the club bunny lifestyle, and we've really taken to her.

I look around the room and I see Clean motor boating one of our newer recruits, Georgia. He's having a ball, but I can see from the look on her face she's annoyed. The club bunnies no better than to talk about any of the patched members, but there are rumors that Clean isn't as well-liked as he thinks he is. The man swears he's God's gift to women, but honestly, he's just an immature pretty boy. His loyalty, strength, and optimism are pretty much the only reasons Prime even deals with him. He's a fuck-up, but his loyalty can never be questioned.

. . .

MY EYES JERK to the side as Cherry starts to saunter in my direction, I know what she wants, what she always wants. To fuck. As much as I love fucking her until she's whimpering and damn near passed out from coming so many times, I'm just not in the right mind frame for it tonight. Our rough fucking might get a little too rough, and I'd never want to truly hurt her. I wait for her to come closer and wrap her arms around my neck. She slides her curvy legs between mine, but before she can say anything I speak, "Not today Cherry, Wire was looking a little pent-up earlier. Check on him when he and Gin get back. "Come on, Alex, you look so stressed out. You know you can take it out on me…" She leans further in and licks the shell of my ear, "as hard as you want to."

My cock pulses to life and I feel my hand slide over to her hip and squeeze. Maybe a quick fuck is exactly what I need.

"There he is." She purrs and just as I'm about to pull her towards my room, the front doors to the clubhouse burst open.

I see Gin's bald head over the crowd and Wire not far behind him. They look like they're on the move. Walking as if they have something to share.

"Not now." I say again to Cherry and push her back. She doesn't complain, Cherry knows when club business is going on she's to be scarce. I make my way towards the two of them, Prime isn't one for the parties, so right now I'm in charge as the VP. Whatever they found out, I want to know.

"Alex, you not going to believe this shit!" Gin says over the loud music.

I put my hand up to stop him, I'm not going to strain and give myself a bigger headache because I'm trying to hear what he has to say over the loud music. Church is soundproof for a reason.

I look at Wire who has that glassy look in his eyes, his shirt is splattered with blood. "Wire, you good?" As our enforcer, Wire is one of the coldest motherfuckers I've ever come across. He's always good, but I need to make sure before I dismiss him.

"Yeah. I'm straight. I'm going to get a drink." He nods and then walks off.

"Come on." I gesture to Gin so he can follow me. We get into the church, and before I can even get the door closed, he's talking.

"You're not going to believe this shit, or you might. It's who we thought, the fucking Rolling Cobras are behind this shit. I knew all that talk with Prime was bullshit. We should've taken them out when we had the chance."

I put my hand up to stop him, "Wait, how the fuck do you know this shit?"

"How you think? I'm really starting to think there's something mentally wrong with that bastard Wire. We cornered one of the Rolling Cobra prospects and your enforcer did what he does best, deliver pain. The prospect was squealing like a pig within five minutes."

I run my hand through my hair and turn to walk away. The last group I want to go to war with right now is the Rolling Cobras, not because they're stronger than us, but they're reckless. They'd have no problem walking into a public place and just shooting up the place to get to us.

We can't have them making a mess in town or hurting anyone just to get our attention.

"How do we get their attention? I don't want this turning into a fucking shoot out in the local coffee shop." I look over to Gin, who is smiling at me like a fucking hyena.

"That's the best part about Wire, not only does he get them to talk, but he gets them to spill all the secrets. They made another drop out here and are coming to pick up in a few days. We can be ready for them." He rubs his hands together, and it dawns on me that he's fucking impressed with himself.

"Why you so fucking proud? You should have known about this shit weeks ago. We should've been able to stop this from happening." I glare at him and that smile drops off right away.

"Yeah, I know Alex I just…"

"Shut the fuck up, I don't want to hear it, Gin. Get your shit, together. If you can't get the fucking information that we need, what do we need you for?" I peer at him for another second before I turn and walk out of church. Now, we know who the enemy is, we need to get ready for him.

CHAPTER 3

Alex

"Are you fucking sure that they said today? Maybe the kid was lying." Prime says as we hunker down even further behind cover. Today is the day the prospect told Wire the Rolling Cobras were supposed to come back to pick up another package they left at the edge of our property.

"Well, I can't really ask him seeing as he's fertilizer now, but the steel nails through his hands made me think he'd be as forthcoming as possible." Wire says deadpan.

"Through his hands? What the fuck." Ryder grimaces and shakes his head, but keeps his eyes on the prize.

"Prime if Wire got time with him, the information is right." I look over, there's no way that the dead prospect lied to Wire. I've never seen someone hurt anyone as bad as Wire can hurt people. The kid has a fucking gift.

"I know, but—"

We all shut up as the sound of motorcycle engines start to get closer to us. It's the dead of night, there should be no one coming this way, and especially not this many. I put my hand on my gun and do my best to stay calm. I don't want to pop up too soon and give away our position. We need to figure out exactly where they stashed the drugs so no one else comes around and tries to do the same thing.

A group of five men come to a stop no more than fifty feet in front of us. Instantly they start digging. Wire and his victim were right.

"Alex, you got my six?" Prime turns his head in my direction and I give him a quick nod. Shit is about to go down, and I'm ready for it.

"Don't you fuckers think it's a little too late for a neighborly visit." Prime barks out, catching the trespassers off guard. Max, Wire, Ryder, Gin, Archer and I are all still in cover with our guns ready. Prime is at the edge, peeking out from behind the brush.

"You stupid motherfucker. You should have left us the fuck alone!" I can't tell who it is on the Rolling Cobras, but from their kuttes I know it's them. Before Prime can say another word, bullets start flying in our general direction. They don't know exactly where we are, but they do know that we're here for them.

Archer crawls over, and I watch as he leans his head out ever slightly and fires one shot. His target goes down quickly, a shot right between the eyes. I don't know why we don't just let Archer and Wire loose on these assholes and go home for a beer. The two of them could manage them no problem.

Just as I lose myself in my thoughts for a second, a bullet cracks against a branch above our heads. I hear the ominous groaning and snapping right before a large tree limb comes crashing down over us.

"Shit!" Ryder and the rest of the guys dive out of the way, but Prime is still focused on the Rolling Cobras.

"Fuck! Prime move!" I push him out of the way and groan as the large branch comes falling on my leg.

"Motherfuckers!" Prime roars and tries to dislodge himself from under me and the tree.

I kick my legs and finally get the branch off the two of us, pulling Prime and me back into cover just as more bullets come in our direction.

"Wire! Boy, what the fuck are you doing?" Prime yells out, but Wire is already on the move. In his fog, not giving a fuck about life. I swear one day this man is going to get shot walking through the fucking fire like he's invincible.

"Wire! Get the fuck back in cover!" I yell at him, but he pays me no mind. He won't. Once Wire is gone, there's no getting him back.

I push Prime towards the center of the cover, but that doesn't stop him from scurrying over to the other side. He opens fire, and before we have a chance to understand who is here from the Rolling Cobras, my club has already outflanked them and has taken them all down. No casualties on our side, and we still have the drugs that they buried.

As a club, we might not allow our members to use, and we don't deal, but we'll trade or deliver for a fee. This amount looks to be at least double what we found before, so it'll bring in a nice chunk of change.

"Wire, Gin, Alex. You three get rid of these bodies. I wish we could've left someone alive, but check their bodies and…ugh." Prime stops talking and presses a hand to his chest like he's in pain.

"Prime, you good?" Archer steps forward.

He clenches his eyes closed for a second before he opens them again, "Yeah, I'm fucking straight.

"You sure? You're sweating." I step closer. He doesn't look good at all.

"What the fuck do you think I'd be doing we were just in a fucking shootout. You think I'd be dry as the Sahara? Jesus, Alex, get your head out of your ass and make sure these guys get rid of this shit. Find out what we need and then get back to the clubhouse. I'm going home." Prime barks at me, and even though I can tell he's trying to be tough. I can see the pain. Something is going on with my president.

"Yeah, Prez, I got it." I say. He knows he can trust me with anything. As the VP, it's my job to make sure everything is handled if my president can't be there to do it.

Prime nods tightly once before he turns to walk to his bike. I cut my eyes to Ryder and Max. "Go with him." I mouth and they rush to catch up. I don't want something happening to Prime because he's too fucking stubborn to realize that he can't do this shit on his own. None of us can.

"WHAT THE FUCK, man, are you going to dig any fucking slower?" Gin complains.

"Maybe if your ass worked out every once in a while, you wouldn't be so fucking out of breath." Wire snaps at Gin. Wire is one of the younger members, but he's not afraid to say what's on his mind, no matter who it is. Gin is big enough to give Wire some trouble, though I've never seen the kid lose a fight.

"Shut the fuck up, both of you. Get this shit done. I want to get back to the clubhouse, so we can figure out the next steps." I order them.

"What do you mean the next steps?" Archer asks.

"I mean, these motherfuckers are not just going to stay back and forget that we took out five members of their crew. The Rolling Cobras are going to come for revenge. We need to be ready for it."

"Ready for it? Alex, honestly, I've never met anyone who's tried to control as much as you. There's nothing that we can do now. Those assholes know we took out their men and if they come, it's not like they're going to be ringing the dinner bell as they ride down the fucking road. You try to micromanage everything, it's just going to piss people off." Gin shrugs and continues to shovel.

"I'm not trying to control shit besides keeping us alive. If you can't fucking appreciate that shit, than why the fuck are you here?" I sneer at Gin.

"Alex, I'm not trying to disrespect you. You're my VP, but I think Gin might be right with this one. What the fuck can we do? Are we going to lock everyone down and just wait for one of them to show up, so we can get rid of them? How do we know that they aren't somewhere watching us right now? There's just some shit that we can't control." Wire says, leaning on the end of his collapsible shovel.

"I don't give a fuck about going into lockdown or pissing people off. I don't care about who's watching us or if they let us know. All I give a fuck about is staying alive and keeping my brothers alive. If I have to piss off every one of you, that's what the fuck I'm going to do." I spit out.

"Well, I don't know how to tell you this, Alex, but that's not your decision. Last I checked, Prime is the president." Gin smiled before he continued to shovel. Archer and Wire follow along, leaving me to fume at his remark. He's right, I can't put any of the precautions in place like I want. I have to wait for Prime to give me that directive. I only pray that he sees shit the way I do.

CHAPTER

Alex

It's been days since we had our firefight with the Rolling Cobras, days, and no retaliation. I feel like I'm going out of my mind here. Like they're just waiting around the fucking corner, but Prime doesn't see it that way. He's making it seem like they've learned their lesson, and they're not going to come fuck with us anymore. I never want to think my president is incapable, but shit like this makes me feel like maybe he needs to reevaluate what the fuck he's doing here.

"You ever going to get that stick from up your ass?" Max comes and sits down next to me. He's been at the club since I have. He's my brother and the only one besides Ryder and Prime that truly understands me.

"Shut the fuck up, Max. Seriously, how the fuck can everyone be sitting here all fucking happy we've gotten some free drugs to sell back?" I cut my eyes over to him. I just can't understand why this isn't a bigger problem for everyone else.

" First of all, Prime says we're okay. He said there's no

reason to think the Rolling Cobras were going to come back now. I mean, they have to know we're going to be coming for them if they try to drop on our land again. The drugs were a huge pay day for everyone here, and honestly, we're all fucking tired of fighting. If Prime thinks we can be in the clear for once, then fuck it. Let them stay over there with their tails tucked between their legs, and we can be over here partying our ass off." Max stretched out on the lounge chair next to me.

"Max, you know this shit isn't over." I say, looking him in the eye and hoping I have at least one person in here that can see what I'm talking about. That there's at least one person here that knows we're all probably still in danger.

"Alex, I know brother. Yeah, but until something else happens we need to celebrate the small victories, or we're not going to make it through. Look at the new stages we got for the parties. Did you see the security system Archer brought? What about the new furniture for our rooms? All that shit is possible because of this win. Let's focus on that shit for a little while instead of waiting for the next shoe to drop. When and if the Rolling Cobras come back, we'll be ready for them. There's no fucking use being anxious about it now." Max says and tries to get up.

"Wait a minute, I'm not fucking anxious." I snap at him.

He chuckles and then drops himself back on the chair. "No? Tell me, how often are you thinking about the Rolling Cobras coming in here and starting some shit with one of us? Do you have an idea as to where they would come from? Do you think you'd be able to get us out? Who do you think would die first?" He asks quick fire questions, and my mind reels as I get ready to reply. "Do you have answers for all those questions?"

"Yeah, of course. And if we could just buckle down tighter, we could make sure nothing happens. We'd need more weapons. Or even some sort of incendiary device—" He cuts me off from saying anything else.

"Alex, that's the fucking definition of anxiety. Worrying about shit that hasn't happened or may not ever happen. And from the way your pupils are dilating, and you're breathing, it looks like you got more fucking anxiety than the rest of us. You need to relax." Max shrugs slightly before he gets up from his chair, leaving me there dumbfounded.

I'm not fucking anxious.

My eyes scan the crowd and I settle on Mick, He'd be the first to go. He can't run.

The door is a heavy wood …it'd be easy for them to break it down with a car or a… "Fuck!" I jam my hand in my hair and tug. "He's right, I'm fucking anxious about some shit that hasn't even happened yet. I need to get myself under control and worry about what I have to do now and not shit that might happen later.

ALMOST THREE DAYS after Max pointed out to me I'm a little more wound up than most, nothing has yet to happen. Maybe the Rolling Cobras really have learned their lesson.

"Bullshit! You can't hit that target and even if you could, it wouldn't be a bullseye."

Clean and Archer had a bet going on about Archer being able to hit the dartboard with his knife with a blindfold on. I don't know what kind of superpowers Archer has, maybe some voodoo or magics from his hometown of New Orleans, but the man has never missed a fucking shot. I don't know why Clean would take that fucking bet.

"If you don't think I can hit the target, why wouldn't you put up your po'boy?"

"Because I rode nearly thirty miles to get the fucking sandwich. It's mine. I want it."

"Fine, then admit I can make the throw." Archer waves his hand weakly as if he doesn't care.

"You already had one sandwich, Clean. You greedy asshole." Wire is leaning against the bar with a half smirk on his face watching the two of them bicker with each other.

"What do you think Wire? You think he can make it?" Clean turns to look at his best friend, and Wire squints his eyes.

"You have to question that? The man is one of the best sharpshooters in the world. The entire world, Clean. You think he'd miss a target not more than 30 feet away just because he can't see?"

Clean nods his head and rubs his chin like he's in deep thought. "You're on."

I slam my hand to my forehead as does Wire, Mick, and Max. I love the kid to death, but Clean isn't the sharpest tool in the shed.

Archer throws his head back in laughter before he turns towards the dartboard, takes a few steps back, and allows Clean to tie a piece of cloth over his eyes. He doesn't even bother to look at the dartboard again.

Hell, none of us have to look at the dartboard. There's not one person in here besides Clean who thinks Archer's going to miss. There's just no way.

Archer stills for a second. "Am I clear?"

I look toward the wall where he's about to throw the knife. That would be fucked up if someone was to walk by just as he throws the knife. He'd never forgive himself for that shit.

"Yeah, you're straight." I tell him, and he quickly flings his knife straight at the wall. The knife hits the bullseye so hard it cracks the board in two, and it splits directly in the center, causing it to fall to the ground.

"Motherfucker! That doesn't count!" Clean yells out as we all start to laugh at him.

Archer rips the blindfold off, and I can see the look of confusion on his face.

"What happened? Where is it? What's going..." He looks down to the floor and sees the board there. "Don't welch!" Archer walks over to Clean with his hand held out, waiting for his winnings.

"Bullshit! I said if you hit the bullseye!" Clean tries to argue.

"Hey asshole, he did hit the bullseye. He hit it, then went through it, then he fucking broke it! You lost Clean, give it up." I joke with them.

"You bastards finish playing your fucking games, or should I wait here for another ten minutes while you get your shit together?"

I swiftly turn around to see Prime leaning with his foot up and braced against the door of the church. His arms folded across his chest.

"Shit. We didn't even know you were there." I say and start walking in his direction.

"I need everyone. Church. " He calls and Max, who is SAA, starts walking too. Clean, Archer and Wire stay out since they don't usually come in for church. Even as the enforcer, Wire isn't considered one of the higher ups yet.

"No, everyone. This business affects us all." Prime says, and instantly that heavy stone I've been trying to ignore in my gut flips, twisting my insides up with it. Something is wrong. Something major is happening. What I don't understand is why the fuck I don't know about it. As the VP, if something was going down then I should be one of the first people to know. When I walk into the room with everyone else behind me, I see Ryder and Mick in the church already. There's a bottle of Jack on the table, and they all look like they've been drinking.

"Prez, what's going on?" I ask.

"It's the Rolling Cobras, isn't it?" Clean says. The jokes and immaturity melted away from him the second he walked through the doors of the church.

Prime falls into his seat and scrubs a hand down his face. The man looks tired. He lets out a long sigh before he starts talking. "You know, when I started this club, it was just me, Mick, and a few other degenerates trying to find a way to make money and stay off the fucking streets. I had no idea what this would become and what it would mean to me and my family. I had no idea that I'd find my fucking home here.

I'd rather die than see anything happen to this club or any of you. And if I stay on as the Prez, that's what's going to happen. I'm too old, I'm too conflicted. I just want to move down to Florida and be with my daughter and grandchild. I'm so focused on the peace and quiet, I don't see the war brewing right in my face. I'm no longer suited for the chair. As of today, I'm stepping down as President of the Wings of Diablo club."

A deathly silence slams into the room. He looks at me, pride and fear pouring out of his eyes. "Alex. Prez, this is now your family to lead."

"What the fuck is going on? Is this serious?" Gin is the first one to speak up. It sets off the explosion needed for everyone to open up.

"Prime, you can't be serious. How can you just leave?" Archer says.

"What about the club. You disowning the patch?" Clean says.

"Alex isn't ready."

That comment grabs my attention and I look over to Ryder, who's looking down. The man is supposed to be one of my closest friends, but he's questioning my ability to lead already.

"Excuse me?" I say louder.

"Hey! Shut up!" Max barks out, and everyone does as he asks.

I repeat my question and glare at Ryder.

"Alex, I love you. You're my brother and a good fucking man, but you're not ready to take this on.

Shock and anger lace my words, "Who the fuck do you think you are, Ryder? I've been VP for years. Anytime something has gone down, I've been right next to Prime trying to make sure we stay whole. How the fuck can you say that I'm not ready for this?"

"You've been by his side. Yeah, you've always been right next to him. You've never been on your fucking own. This shit isn't you picking up the patch and just stepping into his shoes. This is you having to see every fucking possibility, this is you making decisions for all of us and following through even if it's something you don't want to do. You no longer have yourself to look out for, now your decisions should be about the club, for the club and to help the club. You not ready to do that., I'm sorry, brother."

"Ryder, I hear what you're saying, but I have faith in Alex. And he's not alone. That's what the fucking club is for. You all are going to have his back and when he looks like he's about to crumble, which will happen, all of you will steel your fucking spines and keep him standing tall." Prime leans forward and shoots daggers out of his eyes in Ryder's direction, "Also, you don't have a fucking say in the matter, Ryder. Alex is the fucking president, and his word is law." Prime sneers at his friend.

There's not one more peep out of anyone, not even me. I never expected something like this, not anytime soon, at least.

I clear my throat and look at the man I've considered to be something like a father figure, "Everyone out, let me talk to Prime."

"Sure thing, Prez." Wire is the first one to say before he claps me on the shoulder and walks out. The rest follow, doing the same. I've gone from Alex to Prez in five seconds flat. What the fuck is happening here.

Once it's just me and Prime in the room, he starts to get up from his chair at the head of the table.

"No, it's okay." I shake my head, still not wrapping my mind around the fact that he's going to be leaving.

"Fuck that. You listen to me, boy. Respect is a key part of what drives this club. You never let anyone take your seat. The only time you let someone forget you're the president of this club is when you can no longer be the fucking president. Take your seat, Alex." Prime gets up and gestures to it.

I nod my head and sit in his place.

Adrenaline and testosterone flood through my body as I get comfortable. Fucking hell, this feels good.

"You have anything you need to ask me?" Prime asks standing.

"Yes, I need you to tell me everything. WOD is going to be around for a long time, and I need to know how to prepare my men. I'm never going to be you, Prime, but I love these men with all I have. They're my family, and I'll do whatever I have to in order to make sure that we rise to the top.

Prime nods and sits down in one of the open chairs, "You'll make it to the top, Alex, but you'll fall too. What matters is who you are when you get back up." He scrubs his hand down his face, "I hope you have some time, Prez, because I got a lot of shit to tell you."

CHAPTER 5

Alex

2 MONTHS LATER

"PREZ, I hear what you're saying, but where the fuck do you think the money for that shit is going to come from? All our income streams dried up when Prime left. We need to eat before we need to worry about trying to fight the fucking Rolling Cobras." Ryder grits out.

"Fucking hell. Fine." I lean forward in my chair to think, and Max leans forward as well.

"Alex, we need to get some money in. Right now, those assholes at the Rolling Cobras don't seem to be fucking with us. Let's find some cash." Max whispers to me before he leans back.

I nod and look up. "This is what's going to happen. I have a few leads on some work we can do, but I have to flesh out the details. Clean and I will go up to the city and check on another lead later today. Ryder, you figure out exactly what we need to keep us afloat. Max, make sure the rest of these bastards here aren't just stupidly running through our funds."

"Heard." Max says and waits for me to call the end of church. I swing my eyes over to Ryder who has yet to say anything. As the Treasurer, he's having a hard time with the lack of funds coming into the clubhouse.

"Ryder, you straight?" I squint my eyes. If he's going to fight me, I'd rather he do it here.

"Yeah, I'm good." Ryder says, "I'll do the books again and try to see where we can cut out some expenses." He leans back in his chair and shoots me an ice-cold glance. As long as he doesn't disrespect me, I don't care what he does.

"Great. Get out of here, let's get this shit done." I raise my hand and flick Ryder away. A day after I took on the role of Prez, I asked Ryder if he wanted to be higher in the club, but he refused. All he wants is to control the money, so I'm not really understanding why he has all this animosity toward me.

Max and I watch Ryder leave without saying another word. "You know it's just because Prime left. Ryder's not big on change." Max claps my shoulder before he gets up. The minute I thought about it, I knew there was only one person that I would ever make my VP. Max. I'm glad I have at least someone in my corner.

Though everyone is keeping to the protocol, I can tell they don't think I'm going to be able to handle this. It didn't help that as soon as Prime was out the door, all the perks he had vanished right along with him. I stepped into power just as the shit was hitting the fan. I can't depend on the same connections he had. Not only that, but I have to go out and grind to get everyone's respect. It's no problem. I was groomed to take this seat and now that I have it, I'm not going to let a little work scare me off.

Max and I walk out of church to see Archer, Wire, and Gin in the main sitting area. They look like they're playing a card game or something. "Where's Clean?" I ask, and Wire simply gestures to the kitchen. I should have fucking known.

"Clean! What the fuck, man. Do you have a fucking tapeworm?" I yell out as I make my way to the kitchen. When I peek around the corner, I see him with a huge tuna and jalapeño sandwich in his hand and a half-gallon of strawberry milk in the other.

"Oh, you ready Prez? Hold on. I'm coming." He says and proceeds to shove nearly half the sandwich in his mouth. He quickly swallows three large gulps of the strawberry milk, then does the entire process again. I can do nothing but stand there and stare at him in revulsion. He's going to be fucked up later. Human beings aren't meant to eat like that. "You ready yet?" I snap at him once I get my stomach to settle.

"Mmmhmmph." He grumbles and uses his shirt to wipe the junk from his face. The man is a fucking mess. The only reason we gave him the road name Clean is because he's the sloppiest son of a bitch any of us know. Hopefully, if we keep saying Clean around him, he'll realize that he has to pick up his shit. So far, it hasn't worked.

Clean and I walk out to our bikes, passing Gin and Crystal, one of our club bunnies. "You alright Prez, you need more backup?" Gin asks, ready to push the woman away from him and hop on his bike with us.

"Nah, stay here. It's just a bar, no affiliation with anyone we have problems with." I tell Gin. I'm not completely sure that there is no affiliation, but I don't want them to think now that I've become the president, I can't stand on my own two feet. Gin smirks at me, but he doesn't say another word. He's another one that doesn't think that I'm ready for this position. He may not have said so, but I can tell with every fucking glance that I'm right.

Clean and I set out on the road, and we make it to the bar in less than twenty minutes. Hector owns a small niche bar downtown. It specializes in jazz and live music, along with live interactive shows. From what he says, they're usually pretty entertaining. I have yet to come down here and see one. The problem is he's so far downtown that he's been ripped off quite a few times, and he just doesn't have the funds to keep replacing his equipment.

"I just need someone to keep those bastards away from the bar and my patrons. That's all." Hector says.

"Yeah, it seems like a simple protection detail. Nothing crazy." I say and look over to Clean who is sitting at the table with Hector and I. He hasn't said a word since he got here, but his leg is tapping furiously, and he's sweating.

"Clean, you good?" I pat his arm and wait for him to look up at me.

"Yeah, I'm fine." He says, but the muscles in his jaw are locked up, so it comes out harsh.

"Are you sure? You don't look fine. In fact, you look like you might hurl."

"It's fin…" He stops talking abruptly, looks away, and the tapping picks up speed before he looks back up at me. "I'm sorry, Prez." He shakes his head and I squint my eyes.

What's he sorry for?

Just as I'm about to ask him, a loud gurgling sound comes from his stomach and he clenches his hands together on the table.

"What the fuck! You got a fucking alien trying to get out of your guts or something?" I laugh at him. "I knew that sandwich and milk was going to fuck you up."

Clean groans and taps harder. He looks like he's really in pain, fuck, I guess this shit isn't funny anymore. "You need a hospital?"

"Bathroom." He spits out.

"Straight back." Hector gestures and Clean surges up with his hand over his mouth, running in that direction.

For thirty minutes, Hector and I shoot the breeze while Clean vomits and shits his life away. Seems like he has food poisoning, but he's refusing to go to the hospital.

"I'll be good, Prez, just need a few seconds to get my head right. Little dizzy." Clean says weakly.

Hector pushes a glass of juice in his hands, "You should be, you don't have anything left in your system. You're going to need to rest for a little while."

"Yeah, I will when I get back to the clubhouse." Clean tries to get up from the bathroom floor where he's been laying down.

"You think I'm going to let you ride anywhere like this?" I push him back down. "Last fucking thing I need right now is for you to fucking wipe out."

"I have a cot in the back room. It's yours if you want

to take a nap, get some food and drink. You can leave after that." Hector offers.

"That sounds like a good idea. I have to get over to the trailer manufacturer to check on our order, but I can get Wire to come up here and sit with you." I help Clean up to his feet.

"You sure Prez, I can ride. I can do it." Clean tries to tell me, but from the dead weight I'm trying to lift, I know he can't.

"Yeah, Clean. Just get yourself together. I'll be fine riding twenty minutes on my own."

"Okay, a bed sounds nice. Fuck, I'm tired." Clean sways as Hector and I help him to the small cot. He's asleep before his head hits the pillow.

I SHOULD HAVE KNOWN.

Shit always fucking happens when you're alone. I look over my shoulder again and just as I suspected, those guys are still back there. Four guys on motorcycles are about three blocks away. I can't see who they are or if they're a threat to me. They've kept their distance and haven't done anything threatening, so it could just be four people out for a ride. Unfortunately, my anxiety is ramping up big time. I can't call the club and tell them to come guns blazing if I'm not sure, but then again, I don't really want to find out if I'm right.

I look behind myself again and the four of them must be laughing about something because they are still at the light, joshing around. One of them hits the other and throws his head back in what I can only assume is a cackle. I'm being fucking paranoid. They aren't Rolling Cobras, and no one is after me.

I pull off and ride back towards the clubhouse, but I go the long way just in case. The four of them rode in a different direction and just as I'm about to speed back toward the clubhouse the four of them skid back onto the road behind me. Aggressively picking up speed and getting close enough for me to see their patches.

Rolling Cobras.

I should've fucking known.

"Shit!" I hunker down and go faster. I reach into my pocket as best I can, and try to pull out my phone, so I can call for backup. The small cellphone slips out of my hand and onto the ground when they start shooting. "Fuck! You dead motherfuckers!" I roar in frustration, but keep focused on the road. Right now, I need to outrun them.

The way back to the clubhouse is completely deserted, with no usual traffic, so it's just me and them. They've got no reason to back off. I reach to my side and pull my weapon out. I can't afford to aim. I look back for a second and shoot as best I can while keeping the bike on the road.

The four of them easily swerve out of the way and one of them speeds up to get alongside me. He tries to aim his weapon, but I kick his handlebars and get him unbalanced. He tries to right himself but as he's trying to do that, I pull off my lid and slam it into his face, causing him to fly off his bike. The men behind him don't react in time, so instead of going around, they roll over their downed comrade.

They continue to pursue me and instead of someone stopping to check on their man they are focused on me. They're not going to just let me get away.

Another bullet zings by me and I swerve again. More bullets fly in my direction and one hits the side of my bike, causing a loud pop followed by a deep grinding sound to erupt in the air. My speed drastically slows. I look around in a panic for a way to defend myself. I have a gun but there are three of them and one of me. No back up and my bike is about to be out of commission.

I look to the side and I see down the hill, on the other side of a slow-moving brook is a small patch of woods. I know on the other side is a suburban complex. It's a few miles, but I can run it. I have no choice. There's a decline I'm sure I can ride down coming up. At the last second, I turn my bike and basically skid down the side of the cliff.

My bike twists and groans, but my bitch gets me down safely. If I could promote an inanimate object, I'd give my bike the title of VP, Max would just have to deal with it.

Finally, I make it down to the small rushing water and hop off my bike. It's still early in the day, so It's not like I can hide in the shadows. I have to run.

The second my bike hits the ground, I'm sprinting towards the trees. The water comes up to my thigh, and I'm grateful it's not faster than I thought it was.

"Don't run now, bitch!" Someone screams out from behind me. When I chance a glance, I see they have followed me down the side of the hill and are still chasing me.

I don't bother to reply, I need to save my breath.

Reaching down to my side, I look for my gun, but it's gone. "God dammit!" I bark out at no one in particular. It must have fallen off when I was coming down the side of the cliff.

I make it into the trees and do my very best to stay ahead of them, but they're not giving up. As the trees get more dense, it's harder to see where I'm going. I keep running, and they seem to stay right behind me.

The world spins in the opposite direction as I plant my foot and the earth gives way. I slip forward, and before I can stop myself, the momentum forces my body to roll down a hill I didn't see. I don't know how far up it is. I don't know if there's a free fall. All I can hope for is I fall unconscious before I die.

Trees and rocks jab into my body and I do my best to stop myself. When I realize I'm going too fast to do that, I just pull my arms up to protect my head.

It feels like forever, but shortly after the fall I land with a thud on the ground. I open my eyes and look up through the trees, trying to find the sun.

"He fucking fell! Go down that way! No asshole, that way! We'll catch him before he gets to the town! Hurry the fuck up!" I hear someone scream out in the distance, and my mind clears. They're still fucking coming for me.

"Shit! Shit! Shit!" I roll over to my stomach and quickly do an assessment. I don't know if I fucked myself up from the fall, but right now, I need my body to work with me, so I don't die.

I push up, and my arms ache, but nothing serious. My eyes stay focused, so I'm thinking I don't have a head injury. As soon as I get up to my knees, I have to slam my hand to my mouth to keep from screaming out. Looking down, I see something sticking out of my leg right below my knee.

Fuck, I broke my leg.

I reach down and feel for the bone, but instead of a bone, I feel wood. Just as I hear branches snapping and something rushing in my direction, I grab hold of the wood and yank. It's not a large piece, but it hurts like a motherfucker coming out. If there are any splinters still inside of me, that's going to be a fucking problem for a different time.

Using my other leg to push myself up, I start to run again, but I'm nowhere near as fast as I should be. They'll catch me without a doubt. I need to get somewhere I can lie low. The small suburban complex should be close, but I don't see any houses.

As quickly as I can, I push my way through the rest of the trees and wade through another small brook, only to come through on the other side to see an open field.

"No, no, no!" Searching furiously, I look for somewhere to hide. I came out next to a playing field. On the other side I see a gathering of people. Little kids in neon colors running around kicking a soccer ball and parents on the sidelines screaming at them. Luckily, I'm so far away that they don't notice me. I can't hear the Rolling Cobras behind me, but that doesn't mean that they aren't still looking for me.

I do my best to walk inconspicuously across the field, but I see the kids getting ready to turn back around in my direction. Thankfully, it seems like it's toddlers playing, so none of them are moving very fast.

I make it to the other sideline just as they get to the goal and am instantly surrounded by parents trying to keep up with their children. They'll hide me for a few seconds while I catch my breath.

"Hey, man, are you okay? You look like you need a hospital." Someone says, and just that one comment is enough to get several people to look at me. I don't need a crowd of people bringing attention to me, I need to hide.

"I'm fine, thanks." I grit out and walk away from the crowd. There's a parking lot and I see quite a few cars there. One of them must be open. I don't really want to steal someone's car, but I will.

I look back and sure enough, I see three adults coming out from the tree line. These motherfuckers are persistent as fuck.

I'm bleeding, I'm slow, and I don't have anything to protect myself with. I'm fucking screwed.

Making sure I don't set off any alarms, I quickly sneak around the parking lot, trying to find a car with the door open. I find an old Camry with the back doors open, and I slide in. I have to lie down because the Rolling Cobras have already made it to the parking lot and are looking for me. I cover myself with a dark blanket the person has on their back seat and hope it's enough to camouflage myself.

As I'm worried about being caught, the most amazing smell of spices and citrus fruit hits my nose and my mouth begins to water. It smells like a home cooked meal.

"I know, I know, I'll just pick up the oil and cornmeal and come right back." A woman yells out.

"Please don't be this car. Please don't be this car. Please don't—"

Chirp

"Fuck," I mutter to myself.

The driver's side door opens, and a woman sits in the front seat. She doesn't look behind her, but I know the minute she does, she's going to scream. If she screams, that's it for me. I use the blanket and wrap it around my hand to make it look like I have a weapon and press it to her side.

She jumps in fright and just as she opens her mouth to scream, I reach up and clamp my free hand over her mouth. "If you scream, I'll kill you. Do what I say, and everything will be fine."

Hot tears hit my hand and I look up into the rearview mirror to see fear in her eyes.

"Don't be afraid. I don't want to hurt you. Just keep

quiet, okay?" Making sure to keep her gaze, I admit this to her. She nods her head and I let go of her mouth.

"What...whh... what do you want?" She whispers shakily.

"Just drive. You see those guys searching cars. They're looking for me. Drive me out of here, and I'll let you go."

She looks around at the Rolling Cobras, who have now split up and are still searching the cars. She looks back at me and then back at them before she starts her old Camry up and slowly starts to drive out of her space.

She's going too slow.

I'm too visible.

I try to hunker back down, but it's too late.

Just as she drives onto the lane that goes to the exit, one of the Rolling Cobra's looks inside the car and makes eye contact with me.

I'm fucked. No, we're fucked.

CHAPTER

Laura

"Oye! Ayuda me!" I yell out as I try to pull the large barrel of flour out from under the small sink on the food truck and get stuck in the process. I love working on the food truck, but everything is so small in space that it's almost a full-body workout getting the truck ready for the day.

Drivin' Sol is a project my best friend was so excited about. She talked for years about how she wanted to be a chef and work for herself. Finally, she got a loan and bought an old truck, transformed it into Drivin' Sol, and started the business. Choosing me to be her sous' chef. I was perfect to help her. Everything was absolutely wonderful until about three months after she bought the food truck. It was then she realized she no longer wanted to be a chef.

Now I'm stuck with a college student trying to make ends meet as my sous chef and a job I can never take a day off from. I can't complain much. I love to cook. I've been cooking since I was four with my mother back in Puerto Rico. Something about feeding people has always made me happy.

"Sorry, Laura, I didn't see you down there. Are you all right?" Marisa asks as she helps me pull the large bag out.

"Yeah, I'm fine. I wish we had more space." I grumble.

"You could always talk to Sara and get her to renovate the food truck. I mean, this is hers, after all." Marisa says, right as she goes back to the small prep area and starts to chop up the chives.

"Please. Like she would dump any more money into this hunk of junk." I laugh and turn to the other small work area. The radio is right overhead and I reach up to turn it on. Immediately, I hear an old salsa song by Celia Cruz and I get into my zone. The work moves fast as Marisa and I cook and dance with each other in the small space. The location we're at this morning is full of kids and their parents for the peewee soccer tournament. By the time twelve hits, we're going to have a large crowd. These games always put a nice chunk of change in our pockets.

"Mira! Laura, cuidado!" Marisa screams out just as I turn around. My hip bumps into the small table and a huge jug of oil falls to the ground. The container cracks and the oil goes flying everywhere.

"Shit! Get the flour!" I yelp and we both lunge to get huge scoops of flour out of the barrel and dump it on the floor to stop the oil as best we can. It only takes twenty seconds for the both of us to look like we've been rolling around in the white powder, and the entire inside of the food truck to be a mess.

I look up at the clock on the wall and realize it's only an hour before the kids start coming this way. We don't have much time, and we can't cook like this. "We need to get this cleaned up."

"Yeah, that's a problem, but it's not the *big* problem," Marisa says as she grabs a broom and starts sweeping up the oil-saturated flour.

"What? What's the big problem?" I ask, suddenly looking around for the fire I'm sure we're going to have to put out.

"That was all the oil. We don't have any left to cook with."

My eyes open wide. That's impossible. Utterly impossible. We always have oil here. I did need to get to the store for some more, but I thought we had at least another five-gallon jug here. We deep-fry a lot of our menu items, it's not the healthiest thing in the world, but the kids like it, and it's easier for them to hold. We use oil for pretty much everything. There's no way that I would let us run out.

I slide over to the small storage area and open it up. "There has to be one here! I'm sure of it!" I push the few bottles around in a panic, as if the oil is going to magically appear.

"All this on the floor was from there. The last one. " Marisa says.

Fuck, we can't cook without it. If we can't cook, we can't make money. If we don't make money, Sara is going to sell back the food truck. The fad is over for her, but it's my life. Until we find enough money to buy her out, I have to make sure that this place stays at least a little profitable. It hasn't been as of late.

"Okay, well, I have to go get some. You clean up, and I'll run over to the store and pick up enough oil to get us through today.

"Okay, I'll finish the prep too... oh you know what could be a good treat? We could make some *arepas*. You think you can pick up a small pack of cornmeal?"

"Yum, yes, the kids will like that." I say, already grabbing my keys and wallet ready to hop out.

"Okay, well, hurry back. You know those little stinky monsters will be here soon. I'm worried." Marisa grumbles and I laugh.

I hop out of the food truck and yank my apron off, making sure to wipe off any remaining flour from my person. "I mean it, Laura, I'll hide before I face them alone. " Marisa says to me as I walk away from the food truck.

"I know, I know, I'll just pick up the oil and cornmeal and come right back."

I wave back to her and shake my head at the ridiculousness of the situation. The store isn't far from here. I can go the back way and get there faster. Sure, I hate driving on that deserted road, but it's better than not being able to get to the store. I hit the small key fob on my car to unlock the doors, but it only chirps once, letting me know they're already open. I never lock my doors. Someone is going to steal it one day. Not like it's worth much anyway. I slip into the driver's seat and I pick my key up to start the car when I feel something jab into my side.

I look behind myself for a second and see a man in my back seat. He's dirty, sweating, and he has a gun. I turn back to face forward in shock until I open my mouth, ready to scream. Before I do, he puts his hand to my mouth. "If you scream, I'll kill you. Do what I say, and everything will be fine."

Oh, god. Oh, god! I'm going to die! Oh, god!

My heart feels like it's skipping beats in my chest. I'm so scared. I try to breathe, but it's hard. My eyes water and I do my best to keep as still as I can. I don't know what he wants. If he wanted the car, he could have just stolen it. My life is worth so much more than a triple used car.

Tears stream out of my eyes and I feel him sit up further. My eyes catch his in the rearview mirror.

"Don't be afraid. I don't want to hurt you. Just keep quiet, okay?" He says, his eyes softening with the words.

What? What the hell is he doing in my car if he doesn't want to hurt me?

I nod just so he can let me go. I'm not going to scream, not while he has that gun. "What... whh... what do you want?" I whisper, my voice getting caught in my throat.

"Just drive. You see those guys searching cars. They're looking for me. Drive me out of here, and I'll let you go." He stares at me and for some reason, I can hear the sincerity in his voice. He's not trying to hurt me, but he's in trouble. I can understand doing fucked up shit in order to survive.

I look him over again and can see small scrapes on his face, and finally, I see the way his arms shake. This man is hurt, and those guys are looking for him. He's in my car because he's trying to survive. I have to help. I turn the key in the ignition and the car starts up. I drive slowly, not to draw any attention. The man behind me attempts to hide, slouching further down, but I hear him start to curse softly as we pass one of the men.

"Go, go! Faster. He saw us. He's going to follow you. You have to drive faster!"

" What? Are you sure? They didn't do anything! Are you sure? " I ask, trying not to panic. Already this good deed is proving to be bad for my health.

"Yes! Fucking drive!" The man screams at me and just as I put my foot down on the accelerator, I hear the sound of a car alarm going off. They're stealing some-one's car to come after this man.

"Look, mister, I don't want any trouble, just get out." I speed out of the parking lot and start to turn down towards the main road.

"No! Go the back way, it'll be easier for them to catch you on the main road. I can't just get out, if they catch you, they'll kill both of us. Drive fast. They have a long way to catch up to us, and my clubhouse isn't far. I can get us some help and protection there. " He says quickly.

"Clubhouse? *Aye dios*. You in a racing club or some-thing? *Que mierda*!" I slam my hand down on the steering wheel as I push my worn-down car as fast as it will go.

"Motorcycle club. How do you know?" He asks, glaring at me.

"My brother was killed in a fucking drag racing club. All of you dumbasses have those fucking clubhouses. So fucking stupid." My skin prickles with sweat and anger.

The man reaches up and grabs my hair, causing me to swerve slightly,

"Cuidado con lo que dices" He warns me in my native tongue.

If he wanted me to watch my mouth, maybe he should have chosen a different car to hide in. He groans loud and drops his hands from my hair to his leg. I look back and see him pressing his hands to a wound in his leg. It's bleeding, but not enough for me to think it's life-threatening.

"Where am I going? You have to direct me here." I need to focus on getting to safety, then I can curse him out for dragging me into this.

"Stay on the back road. It's a straight shot. "

"Okay, okay, okay" I repeat myself over and over. The repetition calms me slightly.

"Shit! Fucking hell!" the man curses and scrambles from the back into the passenger seat.

"What?" I screech out, but keep my eyes on the road. These back roads can be dangerous when driving at normal speeds. Driving seventy-five miles on an unpaved road is nearly suicidal with all these twists and turns.

"They're behind us." He says, and I squirm in my seat. "They're going to catch up. Right as I'm about to turn around and look, the back window blasts out and wind and glass burst into the car.

"Ahh! " I scream loudly and pick my hands up to cover my face.

"Are you crazy! Don't let go of the wheel!" The man screams at me before he lunges over to grab the steering wheel. "You're going to get us killed!"

"Me! Are you fucking kidding me?" My voice is so high-pitched if the back window wasn't already shat-tered that would have done it.

Something pings off the car and I look around for the cause. It's gunshots! "Are they shooting at us? What the hell! What did you do to them?" I question and struggle to keep the car on the road.

"Nothing, pay attention! " The man orders me.

I look ahead of me, but this time instead of an open road, two men on motorcycles are coming straight toward us. "Are those your friends?" I ask him.

He doesn't have to answer. His face drains of color and I know it's more of the enemy. Instead of going straight, I drift to the side, trying to get passed them.

One of the men on the bikes quickly U-turns and comes up right beside me. My window is rolled up, but he just uses his gun to break it. I scream my head off, but I don't let go of the wheel. The man in my car reaches over me and pulls the guy halfway into my car. He proceeds to bang his head against the jagged, broken window of my car door. After a few times, the man outside goes limp and my stowaway lets him go.

The car behind us catches up and all at once, it seems like bullets start flying in every direction. But none from inside the car. He lied, he's not armed, which only makes me want to get him away from these bastards more. We're not going to make it to his club-house with them so close to us.

I look to the side and even though I would have never done this on my own, I take a chance. I turn the wheel abruptly, so we ride down the steep hill. My car is more than twenty years old. The engine is fucked up, the transmission sticks, but the frame is solid. I'm hoping that will be enough to protect us. The car groans and thunders as we go barreling down the cliff and into the small stream below. I don't even have time to worry about seatbelts. All we can do is survive. I hope I made the right decision.

CHAPTER 7

Alex

Darkness and pressure surround me.

I try to move, but something has my leg caught. A small hand reaches down and pulls me up. When I look to the side, I see it's the woman whose car I decided to hide in.

"Hey! You awake! We have to get out. The stream is moving the car, we have to move!"

I try to move, but I'm still stuck. A large splash of water slams into the car, and suddenly, I can't breathe again. I wait for a long while for the water to clear, but it doesn't. Finally, after a few seconds, the woman pulls me back up, and I can see her crying.

"You have to help me! Tell me what to do!" She screams at me.

I try to pull my leg again, but It doesn't budge. I blink the dirty water out of my eyes and do my best to get a feel of my surroundings. Looking out the window, I see the trees flying by. The car is in the same stream that was moving slowly just a little while before. Now it's strong enough to push a car with myself and a small woman down the river. There's no massive waterfall or anything that we're going to fall off, but this stream can get very rough. There's no way that we'll make it trapped in the car.

"You have to get out. Climb out and try to swim to shore." I order her and slip back under the water. She grabs hold of my kutte and pulls me back over the water. My weight is pushing the car down on my side. The second she gets out of the car, I'll drown. I'm going to die here today no matter what. I'll be damned if I'm responsible for her death as well.

"What? What about you?" She asks as her hands struggle to keep me up.

"You have to leave me. The river is moving too fast, and this car is just going to keep sinking." I sputter out some water that gets into my mouth.

"No! I'm not going to leave you. You jumped into my car for a reason. I'm supposed to help you." She rationalizes.

"I jumped into your car because it was open. I made a play, and it was the wrong one. You don't have to have the same fate as me. Get the fuck out of here!" I scream at her.

At that second, her hand lets go, and I dunk back under the water. I can't breathe and, in a panic, I try to pull at my leg again.

She grapples for my vest and hauls me back up again. "I'm sorry, that wasn't on purpose. I can't feel my fingers." She shakes her free hand, before she grabs hold of me with that one too. "I don't care what you say. I'm not going to leave you here. Why can't you move?" She asks me. I see the desperation in her eyes and the strength behind that. There's nothing I can say that's going to get her to leave. I know that, even if I don't understand why.

"My leg is either trapped or hooked on something." I try to pull, futilely.

"Is it broken? Or just caught?" She yells just as another large wave splashes into the car. This time instead of bobbing back to the top, the car sinks further on my side. Now she can't pull me back up, and she's under-water herself. Her eyes find mine in the water and I push her away, trying to force her not to die.

She's good. She's everything that's good about my death. I can't let her die along with me.

She pushes herself up and her face rises above the water. Just as my body starts to give in to the lack of oxygen, she pushes herself down to me and presses her lips to mine. She blows air into my mouth and goes back up for air for herself. A second later, she is pulling herself down to where my leg is. I feel her trying to pull and push things where my legs are, but I can't see what she's doing. A few seconds later, she goes back to the surface for more air, but I can see her struggling. Every second that the car is tossed downstream, the deeper we get. She comes back down to me and breathes into my mouth before she goes up and gets more oxygen for herself. She pulls herself toward the back of the car, but I don't know what she's doing. I hate feeling so fucking helpless.

She comes back with something hard in her hand. I don't know what it is, but when she pushes it towards my foot, I realize it's a hammer or mallet of some sort. She shoves it in between my leg and the part of the car that's keeping me pinned. She tries to pull, but I stop her immediately. I can feel the metal, hard object pressing into my ankle. She'll break my leg before she frees me if she does it that way. I point up, and she goes up for more air. She breathes into me and I start to get dizzy being underwater so long and only getting a little bit of oxygen from her. She's giving me mostly carbon monoxide. I'm going to pass out soon anyway.

She gets more air again for herself. This time, when she tries to put the tool in the right space, I adjust it, so she has to push and not pull. She sits with her back to my door and uses her feet to push against the object.

Slowly, I feel the warped metal moving and a few seconds later I can pull my leg out.

There's no time for celebration.

I push her to the other side, so she can get air and try to follow, but the more weight I put in that direction, the more the car sinks. I push towards the back where the window is busted out. She swims out and I pull myself behind her.

My head breaks the surface of the water and I suck in the sweet oxygen. I hear her squeal in fear and when I locate her, I see the current is pulling her away fast. I swim with it and grab hold of her.

"Hold on to my neck. Hold on and don't let go!" I order her and she latches onto me.

I can feel the bottom with my feet.

"Take a deep breath, I need to go under." I tell her and she complies. I take another deep breath and dive to grab hold of the rocks and branches sticking up from the stream floor. The fixed objects make it easier for me to pull us across the width of the stream. This far down, the small brook has opened into more of a rushing river. I have to come up three times before I make it to a point where I can stand and walk. She lets go of my neck and I have to hold her waist to make sure she can get the rest of the way across.

Once we get to the other side of the stream, we fall to

the ground and breathe deeply. She hacks up some water a few times, and part of me is concerned that she might still be drowning.

"Hey, are you okay?" I ask and roll over to her. I put a hand on her shoulder, and she slaps it away.

"No! I'm not okay. I've been shot at, in a car chase, almost drowned, and almost swept away by a fucking river. Nothing about what just happened is okay! This isn't okay. *Tengo miedo.*" She lets her head drop to her hands and cries.

This is my fault, and I feel like utter shit for getting her involved in this mess. If I had known what was going to happen, I wouldn't have done it.

"Hey, you don't have to be scared. They're gone. No one here's going to hurt you now. We made it. We survived, right. I'll make sure you get a new car if that will help?" I move closer to her again and when she doesn't stop crying, I pull her to my chest. I wrap my arms around her, and she collapses against me to cry some more.

"Shhh, *no llores.* We're going to be safe now. We're going to be fine." I promise her, hoping that's enough to get her to stop crying. I lean down and a muted smell of spices and fruit wafts up my nose. "You smell like good food." I say, and she jerks away from me. She blinks a few times before she starts laughing.

"I can never get it out of my hair. I'm a chef."

"Makes sense. Well, chef, what's your name?" I ask her and move back slightly.

"Laura, you?"

"Alex." I reply

"Well, Alex, I have no idea where I am, nor do I know how I'm going to get home. What's the plan?"

Now it's my turn to laugh, "I figured the second you calmed down enough you'd be on your way."

"Nah, you seem more than capable to lead me. Let's go. I'm right here with you." She says, and the words, though simple, strike a chord inside of me.

She didn't have to help me. She didn't have to stay with me in the car. Hell, she doesn't have to stay with me now, but she is. That type of trust, even if she doesn't know she has it, is humbling.

I need to get her to safety. No matter what.

CHAPTER 8

Alex

WE WALK THROUGH THE WOODS AND DON'T GET TO TOWN until late at night. I'm so sore that I feel like my feet will just fall off from all the blisters. At some point during the journey, Laura took off her shoes and began walking barefoot. She said it was better than having the rubber of her wet sneakers rubbing against her heels.

We come out close to two hours away from the clubhouse, but at least there's no Rolling Cobras waiting for us. I hope they think I'm dead. I hope it's a surprise when I show up to kill them, because when I find them, I'm going to take my time ripping them apart. Hell, I might even join Wire in his dungeon, just to make sure I torture them just right.

"Alex, look over there. That place seems to be open." Laura points to a small corner store.

"Yeah, come on. I grab her hand, and slowly we make our way over to the convenience store. I walk in and there are three men in the store waiting to buy some beer and another woman at the checkout line putting in her lottery. Laura walks in behind me and steps off to the side to slip back on her shoes. I watch as the three men look past me and stare at her. One of them licks his lips as if he's going to come over and talk to her.

Does he not fucking see me here? I'm getting real fucking tired of people testing me.

"Something fucking wrong with your eyes? I promise you after the day I've had, I won't have a problem plucking them the fuck out and examining them for you." I reach over and grab Laura, pulling her behind me.

The man staring at Laura the hardest puts his hands up in surrender before he turns back to the counter to wait to pay. The three of them chuckle, but no one says anything to me.

The woman playing lotto leaves the store and I move us a little closer to the cashier. I hear the three of them talking and even though I'm not sure that they are talking about Laura, just the thought sends me into a rage. I have to clamp my muscles down to stop myself from reaching out.

I hold it together and let them pay for their shit, even though I'm aching to fight one of them. The three of them walk towards the door and the man who was staring at her before says out loud, "Hmm, look at the ass on her, too bad she's a dirty girl."

Just what I was waiting for.

I don't even feel Laura pulling me when I charge him.

I grab hold of his collar and punch him two times. One of his friends tries to jump in, but I quickly elbow him across the face before I focus my attention on the man in front of me bleeding from his nose. I grab hold of his throat just to hold him up.

"I fucking warned you. I warned you, and you decided to be a piece of shit anyway. Now your fucking nose is broken. I'm going to give you a chance to apologize to her, or I'm going to pick another bone to break. One that's not going to be so easy to fix." I grab hold of his hand and twist it in an awkward way.

"Shit! I'm sorry. So sorry. I didn't mean any harm." The man says quickly.

I turn over my shoulder and look at Laura, who is staring at me with her arms crossed over her chest. I see why he's so attracted to her. I knew she was pretty when we were fighting our way through the woods and now that I see her in full light, I see just how gorgeous she is. She's a short thing, maybe five foot three inches. She has long light-brown hair and a pair of pouty lips that make the scowl on her face stand out more. Her skin is tan, and her body is out of this world. She has a great rack and my hands itch to squeeze on those thick thighs. I love that she's got a bit of meat on her bones and from the look of the man whose hand I'm about to break, so does he. I wait for Laura to give me the okay and when she nods, I let him go.

"Get the fuck out of here." I sneer at him and the three of them run out.

"I'm sorry you had to…" I stop talking and take another step toward her. She takes a step back.

Now she's scared of me? We walked through miles of forest together. She has my shirt on because she was cold and now, she's scared? "What?" I ask, confused.

"Are you kidding me? What do you mean 'what'? Are you crazy or something? He didn't do anything to me?" She says and gestures outside even though the guys aren't there.

"No, they didn't, but they were disrespectful. That was after I already asked him to stop the shit. In my world, respect is everything. I'm not going to let anyone disrespect you, the same way I won't let anyone disrespect me." I let out a heavy sigh, I might have gone a little overboard, but I'm not sorry for it. I'll tell her I am, though. "I'm sorry I was so violent. I'm usually able to control myself better than that, but after everything today I'm a little on edge.

She relaxes a bit and takes a step toward me. "I can understand that. I'm a little on edge myself. I'm just so tired. I want to get in my bed and go to sleep." She says and rolls her neck.

"Home, yeah. We need to get you home. Where is home?" I ask her. She rambles off an address and I realize it's less than a mile from here. She gets excited when she hears that. This nightmare is almost over.

I feel uneasy leaving her at her house on her own, but what choice do I have. If she wants to go home, I can't force her to come with me to the clubhouse. I convince the store clerk to let me use the phone in the back.

I call a cab to get to her house. On the way there, she cuddles up to my side and closes her eyes. I'm not used to having a woman lay on me, but If she's comfortable, I'm not going to move her. Now that her hair is drying, it seems like the spice and fruit smell is stronger. I lean down and take a deep smell of her. The drive is quick, but she's already sleeping when we pull up to her house.

She lives in a one-family house in a secluded area. When we get there, a large food truck is parked right in front. It's called *Drivin' Sol*.

"Laura? Is that you?" A woman calls out from near the food truck. She's pacing back and forth.

Laura pops up and tries to rush out of the car, but I grab hold of her. I don't know who it is. It might be a trap.

"It's okay *Papi,* that's my friend and my job. I'm the chef in that food truck. It's fine." She smiles at me and I let go of her, believing that she's safe.

My chest tightens with the way she calls me *Papi*. It's a typical nickname for people in my culture, but something about the way she says it makes me want to find gold and lay it at her feet in tribute. She's hot as fuck.

We both get out of the cab and I pay him with the wet twenties out of my wallet. The driver grumbles, but takes the money and the extra tip I give him.

"Aye dios! Laura! Que pasa! Quien es?" A young woman asks as she runs over to where we are.

"We had a bit of an accident and Laura lost her car in a river. She's had a trying day, but thankfully she's not hurt. I'm Alex." I answer, trying to stay polite but also letting her know that I understand what she's saying.

"Yeah, Marisa. I've had a shit day. Sorry, I never made it back with the supplies." Laura says.

"Supplies? Forget the supplies. I'm just happy you're okay. I can take a cab home from here or I can stay. Whatever you want me to do?" The girl says, and I can see the worry in her eyes.

"Take the cab, I'm going to need to drive the food truck until I get a new set of wheels. I'm honestly just going to go inside, shower, and sleep. I think I'm going to only do a lunch serving tomorrow, late lunch at that." Laura laughs with Marisa. They talk to each other for a few minutes while they wait for her cab to show up. Suddenly, I'm starting to feel like the third wheel. I should be heading home.

"Sorry, to interrupt you two. Is there a phone I can use? I just need to call my team and have them come get me."

"Yeah, let's get you inside. Call your friends and get you home too." Laura grabs my hand and pulls me towards her house. I wasn't expecting her to invite me in, I thought her friend would let me use her cell phone.

Marisa kisses Laura bye and turns to walk down to wait for her cab. Laura and I stay at the front door until her friend gets into the cab, and it drives off.

"I'm so glad she didn't demand to stay, I'm too tired for her. She'll want to know everything that happened. I just want to forget it."

"Yeah, I'll be out of your hair soon." I say nodding.

"I don't mean you, silly. You can stay as long as you need. I know you said your clubhouse is more than two hours away now. It's going to take them a while to get here." Laura pulls a key from an overhanging planter and opens the door to her house. The first place an intruder would look. I hate that, but it's not my place to say anything.

"Yeah, but I can just wait out here on the stoop, so you can get some rest."

"Don't insult me, Alex. You need more rest than I do. You can wait inside." She raises an eyebrow at me, as if she's expecting me to go against her. I won't.

Her home is very nicely decorated. Not too cluttered or too colorful. I take my shoes off and instantly regret it. My feet have more blisters than I can count and the minute I release the pressure some of them start to burst.

"Ahh fuck!" I groan through the pain.

Laura rushes over to me and falls to her knees to help me. She huffs out a breath and drops her hands to her lap when she sees my feet. She tsks once before she starts to talk, "*Aye, Papi,* you need more than a ride home. Call them to get you, but while you wait, I'm going to take care of you." Shaking her head again, Laura wraps an arm around my waist and helps me towards the back of the house.

Take care of me? What does that mean? And why am I so open to letting her do whatever she wants to me?

CHAPTER

9

Alex

BEFORE I CAN EVEN CALL THE CLUB, LAURA HAS ME naked and in the shower. She takes my clothes to launder and gives me a washrag to clean up with. I feel uncomfortable as fuck having her do all this shit for me, but any time I try to tell her no she gives me that fucking look. The one that says, I dare you to tell me no. For someone so little, she's scary. Also, I don't really want to tell her no, which is fucking weird.

Just as I finish with the therapeutic shower, she knocks on the door and hands me three large bath towels. I wrap one around my waist and drape the other over my neck .

She's at the door with her eyes closed and part of me wants to tell her to open her eyes while I'm still naked, but I can't embarrass her like that. Besides, I don't know if she's married or anything like that. She's just being nice to me. I don't want to be that much of an ass.

"I'm good now," I tell her.

She opens the door wide and bends down to look at my knee. It'll need stitches for sure but it doesn't feel like anything is torn up inside. We wrap it up, and I barely feel the pain, just a dull ache I'm going to need to take some ibuprofen for.

She runs her hands over my arms and face. "Your wounds look pretty clean now. I don't see anything crazy."

I like the feel of her hands on me, but I'd be lying if I say I don't want to have my hands on her, "What about you? Let me take a look at your cuts and bruises. I got you into this mess, I think I should be the one catering to you." I tell her and take a step forward.

Her breath catches in her throat and her eyes dilate slightly as she lets them roam down my face and to my chest where she gawks my tattoos and muscles. When her eyes drop to my waist, she gasps and looks back up to my eyes.

"I'm fine, I think the worst thing I have is some dirty feet. I'm very lucky." She takes another step away from me and shakes her head to clear it.

"You can sit in the living room, I had to wash your clothes again, they weren't clean. The phone is in the kitchen."

"Okay, thank you again." I say, and she walks into the bathroom, I assume, to take her own shower.

I look down at myself and realize my cock is tenting the towel around my waist. The last thing I need right now is to be thinking with my dick.

I breathe deeply and walk slowly towards the kitchen. The blisters on my feet still ache, though most of them popped in the shower. I pick up the phone and call the clubhouse. The phone is answered on the first ring.

"Wings of diablo." Someone spits out fast.

"Who's this?" I ask, not recognizing the voice right away.

"What the fuck, either tell me what the hell you want or fuck off. I don't have time…"

It's the prospect, Larry.

"Larry, mind your fucking tongue. It's Alex.

"Prez?" He asks, almost as if he doesn't believe me.

"Yeah, jerkoff, you need my social security number or something? Where's Max?" I ask.

"Max? What the fuck. Oh shit, Prez. Everyone is freaking the fuck out. Clean came home without you. Ryder nearly beat him to death. "

"What, what the fuck! Is he okay? Where's Ryder?"

"Everyone is out looking for you. What happened? Are you okay? You need me to come?" Larry asks quickly. He's a good kid, I have no doubt that he's going to pass his prospect run.

"Is there anyone else besides you at the club?"

"No, just me. "Larry answers.

"Then you stay there, give me Max's cell phone number and Ryder's and Wire's. You try to call them too. Tell them I'm looking for them. That I'm okay but just can't get home."

"You sure?" Larry asks.

"God dammit Larry, I told you what I want you to do, stop fucking questioning me. Just fucking do it."

"Okay, sorry Prez." He mutters before he starts to ramble off the guy's cell phone numbers. If they are out looking for me, they're not going to pick up the phone. It's hard as fuck trying to hear a phone ring while you're riding a motorcycle. I wish there was some way for us to get a mic directly in our helmets or something.

The first person I try to call is Max, but he doesn't answer. The next one after that is Ryder, but I get the same result. Wire is the next one I call, and thankfully he answers.

"What?" He barks out.

"Wire, where you at?" I ask, trying to let my voice be heard over the roar of the motorcycle.

I hear his bike squeal to a stop, "Hello?" He says.

"Yeah, it's me, Alex. Where are you?"

"Holy fuck! Prez! You okay? What the fuck happened? What do you need? What the fuck is going on?" He asks just as quickly as Larry did. I've been gone for hours. I can't imagine how fucking upset they were.

"I'm good, a little banged up but nothing serious. My bike is out of commission, and I'm far from home. I need someone to come with the truck and pick me up. "

"Yeah, where at?" Wire asks and I tell him Laura's address.

Something metal bangs behind me softly. When I turn my head, I see Laura has come out of the shower and is pulling out a pot from under the sink. She's wearing a long sleep shirt that goes past her knees. Her long hair is still wet, but it's pulled up from her clean face.

I can't stop myself from eye fucking her as she starts to cook. Shit, she's not wearing anything particularly sexy, but seeing her next to me puts me into overdrive.

"Prez, did you hear me?" Wire says on the phone.

"What no. Say it again." I focus on the call.

"I said we went down to the Tears of Chaos to press them about your whereabouts, we're almost three hours away from where you're at now."

"Is that him on the phone? Is he okay? Where is he?" I hear Gin in the background now. I don't have the patience or mental capacity to talk to everyone right now.

"Yeah, it's fine, just get here. Make sure no one fucking follows you. I don't want any outsiders brought back to this house. You hear me, Wire?"

"Yeah Prez. I'll only take Max in the truck, no bikes."

"Good, make it happen." I hang up before he has a chance to say anything else.

As I hang up the phone, I see Laura cutting up chicken and putting it into a frying pan with some peppers to sauté. She'd only started cooking a minute or so ago, but it already smells wonderful. "You need me to do anything?" I ask after I replace the phone on the receiver.

No, *Papi*, you go out there and relax. Get off your feet. I'll bring this out for you in a few minutes, okay."

I have to fight back a groan at the sound of her calling me *Papi* again.

"Yeah, all right. Thank you for everything."

She simply smiles at me before she goes back to cooking.

I do as she asks and go into the living room. The food doesn't take very long to make, and less than thirty minutes later she comes out with a plate of rice and sautéed chicken.

I put one spoonful in my mouth before she can even get her own food, and it tastes like heaven.

"Oh god." I moan.

"What? Is it okay?" She asks, coming back over to me.

"Oh god." I say again as I shovel another spoonful into my mouth. I have completely forgone chewing and am just swallowing it all. I'm eating like Clean now.

"Alex?" Laura stands in front of me, waiting for my response.

"Woman, what kind of car you want? Benz? Porsche? I don't have the fucking money for it, but after this food, I'll get you any kind of fucking car you want. It's so fucking good." I say before I pick up another spoonful and shove it in my mouth. She laughs and goes to get herself a plate. When she comes out to sit with me, I see that she barely has any food on her plate. After all the activity she's done today, I'd think she'd be just as ravenous as I am.

"You don't like your own food or something?" I ask her, though it's impossible. There's no one in the world who can say they don't like her food. I'd put money on it.

"Of course, I do, but I'm dieting. Portion control. I got to lose like thirty pounds." She shrugs and goes back to eating.

I stare at her for a second just to make sure she's not joking.

"Go get some more food, Laura."

"What?" She tilts her head and looks up at me.

I lean forward and make sure I hold her gaze, "You don't need to lose one pound. You're sexy as fuck and every part of you is exactly where it should be. Don't starve yourself, go get some more food."

"I...you..." she chuckles and pushes her food around her plate, "I could use another scoop of rice.

"Go get it, in fact,"I stand up and grab her plate from her and slowly walk to the kitchen.

"Hey! What are you doing, I thought you were going to take it easy." She rushes behind me.

"I was when I thought you were going to take care of yourself the same way you take care of me. Doesn't look like that's happening. I'll make your plate." I shovel a pile of rice on the plate and two large scoops of chicken.

"Alex, I can't eat that much." She laughs and tries to pull the food away. "You're going to waste it."

I stop and give her the plate. I follow behind her when she goes back to the living room to eat. I polish off my plate in record time, and she offers to get me seconds. I refuse, but go and get some myself. She's not my servant. I can take care of my own needs as well.

After the second plate, I feel like my stomach might explode.

I hear a loud dinging sound, and she pops up from the couch, "Come on, your clothes are dry."

I take her plate and my own and put it in the kitchen before I follow her to the back of the house. There's a small laundry closet near her bedroom, where a stand-up washer and dryer is hidden in a closet. She reaches in, bending over to get the dry, hot clothes for me.

"Holy fuck." I groan and have to look away.

"Alex?" She turns around and calls for me, but I'm too worked up to answer. *"Papi?"*

I jerk forward, lust pulsing through my body, but I stop myself before I get closer to her. "You married?" I snap out and her eyebrows furrow in.

"No. Why?"

"Boyfriend? Girlfriend?" I ignore her question and continue asking my own.

"No and no. Why are you asking?" She puts her free hand on her hip and holds my clothes in the other.

"I'm asking because you keep calling me *Papi* like you want me to make you scream it." Fuck it, if she smacks me, I know I don't have a shot.

"I… Oh." She looks down, but I can see the blush crawling up her neck and onto her face. "You're very forward, aren't you?" She looks up at me through her lashes.

"It's the only way to be." I shoot her a wink. She side-steps me and I let her go into the room.

Your socks were torn up, but I do have a pack of men's socks I picked up accidentally. They've been sitting here for ages." She digs in her draw, again having to bend over. I don't even try to look away from her ass this time. It's fucking biteable.

She stands up, but this time she hisses out in pain and my attention is drawn from how sexy she is to her being hurt.

"What's the matter?" I take a few ginger steps in her direction.

"Nothing, I'm fine." She says and tries to walk around me again, this time I grab hold of her arm and keep her in front of me.

"No, you don't. What's the matter? You spend all this time taking care of a man you barely know. Make me feel welcome. Cook me a culinary masterpiece. Wash my clothes and bandage my cuts, but you refuse to let me take care of you the same way. I don't think that's fair, Laura." I say and take another step in her direction.

"I don't think those eyes are fair, so none of us are getting what we want." She says as she stares at me.

"My eyes?" I've never thought I had incredibly special eyes. They're simple. Brown and I have good vision, but that was the extent of the specialness.

"Yes, it's like you're staring into my soul. Like I'm completely bare for you, vulnerable, open." She shrugs, and I do my best not to let her words affect me. Or let her see that just her presence is doing the same things for me.

"What's the matter, please don't lie to me, Laura." I say and take another step.

"Honestly, nothing's wrong. I did a lot of physical activity, my calf is tight. I'll be fine tomorrow." She smiles at me, but I'm not going to accept that answer. I would have been fine sitting on her stairs, but she brought me in and made sure I was okay.

"Lay down." I tell her and point to the bed.

"What?" Her voice is soft. She's nervous.

"Laura, I know we met under extreme circumstances, and I've done fuck all but put your life in danger. You have no reason to trust me, but it'd make me feel like less of a completely worthless jerk if you let me help you feel better. I can help you stretch your legs, only if you want, though. If you sleep with them tight like that, you're going to have a killer charlie horse in the middle of the night." I have to bite my tongue in order to get myself to shut up.

"I trust you, Alex. I'm an excellent judge of character. Most times." She chuckles before she walks over to the bed and lies down.

I still have just the towel on, so I slip my warm boxers underneath them. I don't want her to be uncomfortable.

On the side table is a bottle of lotion, "Can I use that?" I ask her pointing to it.

"This is your show, *Papi*, do what you want." She teases me and my cock jumps in my boxers.

"I told you about that. Keep it up, beautiful." I lean down and whisper in her ear, which only gets her to giggle.

I grab the lotion and squirt a little in my hand. I start at her ankle and using a strong touch I massage the leg she says is bothering her.

"Oh… Jesus. That's good." She moans, and the cute giggles are now soft moans.

I go slow, making sure to keep my bad knee in a position that doesn't cause me too much pain. I get to her knee and make my way back down. This time, instead of stopping at the ankle, I go to her foot and start to massage. She moans so loud she has to bury her face in the pillow, and my cock is as hard as steel.

It's agonizing. Where the fuck is Wire and the guys, so I can get out of here. I need to fuck, and this woman is torturing the hell out of me.

I finish her leg and set it down.

"Can you do the other? Please, Papi." She looks over her shoulder, her eyes hooded with desire.

"*Aye, Laura, me vuelves loco.*" I groan out and press a hand to my dick. I don't care if she can see me. She has to know she's driving me crazy.

"It's okay. No worries." She tries to move, and I push her back down gently.

"I'm coming, I didn't say no. I'm just not used to a woman getting me this worked up over a foot massage." I joke before I move over to the other leg and proceed to give her another massage. By the time I get to her foot, I'm breathing hard, and my mind is giving me every excuse to pull her legs apart, rip those panties off and slide inside of her.

"All done." My voice is gruff, and she leans up a bit to look back over her shoulder.

"Um, you don't have to. Your hands must hurt... never mind." She says before she ever asks me to do anything.

"My hands are fine. What do you need Laura?"

"That felt so good, you think you could rub my back the same way. I think the crash jammed my shoulder or something." She says, bringing her lip to her mouth and biting it.

"You'd have to take your shirt off." I tell her, letting her know exactly what she's asking for.

"Mmhmm." She turns back to her front and pulls the long shirt off.

"Oh, what the fuck. God damn it." I curse when I see her laying in front of me. Her big beautiful ass is encased in a pair of lace purple boy shorts and her upper half is completely naked. I can't see anything but her back. It's enough. "Laura, you know what you're doing to me. Damn it. God damn it!"

"We can stop. I can..." She reaches over to grab her shirt, but I rip it away and throw it across the room.

"I don't want to stop. If you do, fine, but don't expect

me to be the one to stop on my own." I grab the lotion and squirt a little more into my hands. I do what she asks, but she's moaning so much that my massage just turns into me groping her. I get down to her ass and I use both hands to spread her cheeks apart and squeeze them. I bend down and slightly nip one cheek.

"Aye, *Papi*. What are you doing to me?" She moans out, and I swear it feels like my need for her is strangling me. I force myself to slow down before I lean over and bite the other cheek. Her back arches and I push her up slightly, dip my face between her thighs. I snake my tongue out and lick her pussy through the cloth material.

"Oh fuck, Alex. Don't play with me. I want you. Please, don't tease me." She says and tries to push back. But I don't let her.

"You know what you're asking for, Laura? I'm not going to make love to you, sweet like. I fuck hard and fast. And I don't stop until you come harder and faster than you ever have in your life. I'm sure you want it, but can you handle it?" I ask and when she doesn't answer right away, I think she's changing her mind.

I back off her, and she turns around, showing me her gorgeous breast and desire flushed face. "That's exactly what I want, *Papi*. Give it to me."

CHAPTER 10

Alex

"Laura, fuck." I ground out before I fall on top of her and steal the very breath from her mouth with a kiss.

She moans and wraps her arms and legs around me. She grinds down, trying to race to her orgasm.

"Don't rush, Laura. I'm right here." I pull back and tell her.

"I don't like to wait. I want it now. Now. Please." She's not patient and I can appreciate that. Fine. If she wants to come, I can help her with that. I push her all the way up until her entire back is against the headboard, and she's sitting up. She looks confused until I push her legs apart and lay down between them. I pull her panties to the side and use my other hand to keep her legs open. I lick against her slick slit, and she moans loudly with every quick flick of my tongue. I put her against the headboard for a reason. I don't want her running away. I hear the wood of the bed creaking as she pushes back.

"*Aye, Papi.* Yes. Right there. Please. Please. Please!" She begs, and I swirl my tongue, making sure to stay in the same spot she wants me to. She sucks in a breath and lets out a soft moan as her pussy contracts under my tongue. Her orgasm flushes through her and her body goes lax. I'm not through with her. I pull her panties off slowly and toss them to the floor. I massage her thighs and nip them softly before I go back to her pussy for my second helping. This time, I move faster and dive my finger deep inside of her tight folds.

"Oh god, you're going to make me come again." She whimpers and I finger fuck her faster until I feel her walls clenching with another orgasm. "*Aye, Papi!*" She screams out, and I can't help but smile. I knew I'd get her to do it.

Her legs tremble as I keep them apart, and she sucks in deep breaths. "My love, do you have condoms."I ask, knowing once I get balls deep I'm not going to want to pull out.

"Hmm? Mmhmm." She points in the direction of her nightstand, and I crawl over to it. I open the drawer and all the way in the back, covered in dust, is a fresh box of condoms. They must have been here for a long time.

The savage inside of me, the one that wants to claim her as all mine, is happy about that.

I quickly break open the pack, pull one of the condoms out, and lay it on the bed.

"*Papi*, I need you again." Laura whimpers out. Turning my head to her, I see her eyes closed and her hands snaking down to her cunt.

"So impatient. You can't wait for me, Laura?" I play with her as I take the towel and my fresh boxers off.

"No. I can't help myself." She admits, and I push myself back up the bed.

"While I'm here, I take care of you. I want all your orgasms. I want all your pleasure. I want all of you, Laura." I press a kiss to her mouth swiftly before I slide down and kiss right below her ear.

"Take me, *Papi*. Take what you want." She moans in my ear and my hips surge up on their own.

I bring my lips back to hers, and she dives her hands into my hair, tugging hard as I wrap my arms around her. I hold her tight as I feel a part of my soul connect with hers through our passionate kiss. That must be my body's criteria to say fuck it all because I press the head of my cock against her wet pussy and slowly thrust forward.

Condomless.

"Fuck." I groan out against her mouth. All the synapses in my brain fire and I'm so overwhelmed with pleasure that I know the minute I sink all the way in I'll be forever lost.

"Oh, Alex. I've never… feels so good." Laura sways her hips and tries to move down on my cock. I have to hold her still because I don't want to come.

"You're so wet and tight. Fucking perfect." I grunt and push even further into her. As I get half way, her head pops up from the bed, and she looks down. My cock has that effect on many women, and I'm not just saying that because I'm big, but because along with the length, I have a subtle curve to my dick. Nothing disfiguring, but I tend to make women tap out if I go too hard.

"More, *dame mas Papi*." She whispers, but she doesn't look up at me; she's watching my cock disappear into her.

Once I'm deep inside of her, balls to her ass, she rolls her hips. It's like a starting gun, and I buck into her like a depraved animal.

Her core wraps around my cock like a glove. The sound of skin slapping against skin and the sloppy wet, slick sound of me thrusting in and out of her has fireworks exploding all over my body.

Her moans and screams for me urge me on as my body fights to keep my orgasm at bay.

"Again, oh god, again, *Papi*." She grabs hold of my

arms and digs her nails into the skin. I don't care if she rips my flesh from my bones, as long as she lets me keep fucking her.

Right as I feel myself about to come, I pull out and flip her to her stomach. I want to come on that beautiful ass of hers. I slide back but this time instead of being able to take my thrusts she's crawling away.

"Oh fuck! You're so deep. Alex, god!" She yells and tries to move away again. I follow her, ensuring I stay deep inside of her. After a few more seconds of this, just when I think she's about to tap out, she widens her legs and arches her back deeper. I slam into her, thinking she's going to move away, but instead, she just whimpers and fucks me back. She meets every one of my thrusts with one of her own, and that small thread of control starts to unravel quickly.

"Shit. Laura. Stop, fuck. Don't!" I warn her, but it does nothing but make her fuck me harder. My eyes roll back, and I feel my balls pull up to my body.

I'm coming. I'm coming so hard it feels like my heart is completely compressed with all the pressure. I throw any caution I had to the wind and reach down for her neck. I grab her, yanking her up, so she's sitting on my dick. Her back to my front. I slam her down furiously over and over, squeezing her next and snarling in her ear. No words, just grunts and pants.

"Papi." She whispers and her body goes stiff as she shakes and squirts all over my lap.

"Mine. You're mine!" I grit through my clenched teeth as I slam up as far as I can and come deep inside of her.

She moans loud, and her body gives out. She falls forward, and I follow, not wanting to pull out and waste one drop of my cum. I press harder, and she whines as my body weight presses her into the mattresses.

I turn my head to the side to suck in some air. My eyes fall on the still wrapped condom on the bed. I reach over and flick it to the floor. No way I'm going back.

I met Laura today.

She hid me. She saved me. She ran with me. She served me. All for no reward.

I may not be a prize, but she has all I can offer. She has all of me.

When I look back on this fucked up day, all I will remember is that I met Laura today.

My Laura.

CHAPTER 11

Alex

DREAMS OF PEACE AND HAPPINESS SWIRL THROUGH MY mind. I've never been so fucking satisfied in my life. Is this what people mean when they talk about soul mates and shit because I believe it. Laura and I explored each other's bodies until both of us were so exhausted we fell asleep. I hear my heart pounding in my ears as I pull her closer to me and fall deeper into sleep.

Laura jerks awake in my arms and the second I feel her body go taut with fear, my eyes spring open.

"What is it? What's wrong?" I croak out. She's gripping the sheets so hard her knuckles are white. She has them pulled up to her chest and she's staring at the doorway.

"Laura! What's wrong?" I try to break her out of the state she's in, but she doesn't say anything. Loud banging sounds and she flinches hard. The door, that's what we're hearing. She must be absolutely petrified that someone from the Rolling Cobras is coming for her. I did this. I made her feel like this. Fuck, I feel like an ass.

"Hey, Laura, look at me. It's okay, it's probably just my brothers. I'm going to check." I tell her and try to get up from the bed.

She grabs hold of my arm, stopping me. "What if it's them, do you think they could have followed me?"

"No, they don't know who you are, but even if it is them, I'm not going to let them get to you." I swear to her and hope that she believes me. She stares in my eyes and nods her head once before she lets me go.

I quickly throw on my boxers and my pants right as the person bangs on the door again. I wish I had my gun, but I don't, so I go into the kitchen and pull out a steak knife. Another round of banging and if it is one of my men, I might just stab him because they fucking deserve it for scaring Laura like this.

I look through the small window on the side of the door just to see who it is. Fucking Max. I see him raise his hand ready to bang again.

I rip the door open before he has a chance.

"Bang on this door again, and I'll fuck you up myself." I snap at him.

He jumps back, startled. "Oh shit! Prez! What the fuck happened, Alex." He steps in the house and pulls me into a hug I wasn't expecting.

He lets me go and takes a step back outside. He whistles and Wire comes out from around the corner.

"What the hell were you doing back there?" I ask when he gets closer.

"I was going to break in and kill people. Thought maybe you were hostage. I'm thinking that's not the case unless that pretty woman in the bed is keeping you hostage and if so, do you really want to be free." Wire smirks and I realize he was just spying on Laura. My fucking Laura.

I raise the steak knife I still have in my hand and press it almost flat against his kutte.

"Wire, brother, I'd give my very life for you, but if you ever fucking look at her again, I'll gut you. Understand?"

His body stiffens, but he doesn't show signs of fear. Wire doesn't scare easily, instead he simply nods and apologizes, "My bad Prez."

I move the knife and focus back on Max. "Did you have any trouble? Anyone following you?"

"No, we made sure and doubled back just to be triple sure." Max replies.

"Good, let me get my things, so we can get home. Stay out here and make sure that no one pops up." I order, and the both of them turn to stand guard.

I do my best to quickly grab up my things before I go in the room to get the rest of my clothes.

"It's your friends, right?" Laura asks. I can still see the fear on her face. What happens when I leave? I can't leave her alone to be scared. I don't want to leave her at all. She needs to be with me. I need her with me.

"Yeah, everything is fine. I need you to get dressed."

She tilts her head, "Oh, how come? I thought you said everything is fine?"

"It is, but you're coming to the clubhouse with me." I say, grabbing my shirt and slipping it over my head.

"What? Why? I don't need to come with you." Her eyebrows press in together, and she shakes her head.

"Yes, you do. This time it wasn't them, but I don't know about next time. I can't tell you with a hundred percent certainty that none of the Rolling Cobras will come here looking for you, and there's no way that I'm leaving you here alone with less than perfect odds. I know I'm high-handed and overwhelming, but I know what I'm doing. I promise you that while you're with me, I'll do everything in my power to make sure you're safe. Once we get rid of this threat, you can let me know what you want to do." I say, shoving my hands into my pockets and waiting for her to make the decision.

"Okay, I'll come." She says quickly.

That was easier than I thought it was going to be. Either she's much more scared than I thought she was, or my powers of persuasion are off the charts.

She chuckles when she sees the look on my face. "It's like I told you back in the woods. I know you have what it takes to lead me. I'd be dumb not to take you up on the offer." She shrugs before she walks over to her closet and starts to get dressed. Once she's done, she packs a small overnight bag, and we walk out of the house to the truck. Max and Wire look at me like I'm nuts, but neither say a word. I get in the back seat with her and we both fall asleep on the way back to the clubhouse. I'm safe with my brothers, and she's safe in my arms.

ONCE WE GET BACK to the clubhouse, Ryder is the first one to stop Laura at the door.

"Prez, what is this?" He points to her, not even bothering to ask her who she is.

"Let me get her inside, and then we can all talk about it."

Ryder blocks both mine and her path again, "Get her inside? You know we can't, unless she's a bunny, and she intends to hop my dick next." He turns her gaze back to her. That same rage I felt in the convenience store bubbles back to the surface. Before I know what's going on, I'm swinging my fists into Ryder's face.

Who the fuck does he think he is? How dare he talk to her like that. She's mine. No one fucking talks to her like that.

I feel only one set of arms pulling me, small and petite. Laura.

I let her move me only because if I don't, I'll hurt her. My eyes never leave Ryder, who is on the floor looking up at me in anger.

"*Papi*, look at me." Laura talks, but instead of panic or anger, her voice is soft and soothing. "Please." She says again, and my eyes reluctantly drop to hers. The anger I felt moments ago towards Ryder dissipates more every second I'm looking into her eyes. "It's okay. You know he didn't mean it. Your friends wouldn't do that to me, right?"

"No, he wouldn't. He didn't know." I reply right away. My voice just as low as hers. It's like she is my conscience, but in the flesh. Ryder is only acting in his normal asshole way. It's true that any women brought into the club unless it's a party are club bunnies, and club bunnies are for everyone's use.

Laura isn't a club bunny and never will be.

"I'm good. Let's get you inside." I tell her and pull away from her grasp. I walk over to Ryder, who is now sitting on his ass on the floor. I put my hand down to him, and he grabs it, so I can help him up. It's as close to sorry as I get before, he turns to walk into the clubhouse. I brought Laura in and set her up in my room. Once I'm satisfied, she's comfortable, I go back out to face my club.

Clean is by the bar, and he looks at me with worry in his eyes. He was the last one to see me before all this shit went down. It does look like Larry was exaggerating about Ryder trying to kill Clean, but not by much. Clean has a shiner, and it looks like he got cracked upside his jaw based on the bruise and the busted lip.

"We can talk out here, what happened earlier concerns everyone."

Gin is the first one to step up, "Can we talk about what happened just now? Who's the broad?" He says and points to my room. The dumb fuck didn't he just see what happened to Ryder.

I take a step in his direction, but Max is the one to reply.

"She's not doing anything to anyone right now. Prez knows why she's here, and that's all that matters. Now shut the fuck up and let your president speak." Max snaps at Gin. Gin looks from him to me and then shakes his head. He moves back, though.

"I'm assuming you all know by now that I had to leave Clean back at the bar because he had a tummy ache." I shoot a glance at Clean, who grimaces and drops his head down in embarrassment.

I snicker slightly before I continue, "You're good Clean. This wasn't your fault. I made you stay." I refocus and continue with the story. "While I was on the way back, I was chased down by four Rolling Cobras. I killed one of them down by Hutton Pass, but those assholes got a good shot in, and they disabled my bike." I stop and turn to find Larry. "Larry, when I'm done, you, Archer and Barry take the truck and get my bitch." The three of them nod and I continue.

"Once I realized I wasn't going to outrun them on my bike, I jumped the hill and took off by foot. I ran through the brook and into the woods, trying to get to the suburban complex on the other side."

"The complex isn't by Hutton though, it's closer to Lambo pass, that's a mile further." Max says, and I squint my eyes at him.

"I know that shit now, don't I?" I roll my eyes and continue to tell them all about falling down the cliff, ending up in the soccer game, and finally hiding away in one of the cars in the parking lot.

"Let me guess, it was her car?" Ryder asks.

"Yes. Laura. She's a chef and I held her hostage, put her life in danger, and she's been taking care of me like I'm a fucking king ever since. I don't deserve any of what she's done for me and I damn sure am not going to let anyone," My eyes scan the room, so I can capture everyone's attention, "disrespect her. Ever. If it wasn't for her, I'd be at the bottom of the fucking river dead."

Max nods, as do Wire and Mick, but that's all the support I have right now.

"What happened after you guys got safe?" Archer asks.

"We took a cab back to her house and I waited for the calvary." I reply.

"That didn't happen right away. Why didn't you just take a cab home? Why go to her house?" Gin asks the question in rapid succession. "Did you think they were following you or something?"

I don't like all the questions. "What the fuck does it matter, Gin?"

"Is that why she's here? Is she not safe?" Clean asks this time.

"I think she is, but we're going to make sure of it. We hit the Rolling Cobras tomorrow." I announce, and I watch everyone's jaw drop.

"Whoa, whoa, we can't just rush in there now," Archer says.

"You want us to go to war, tomorrow?" Clean questions, his voice raising an octave.

"This is bullshit, you know we don't have the firepower or the funds to get the fucking firepower in order to pull this shit off." Ryder offers up. "This is fucking suicide, Alex."

"You're not thinking this through. This is your dick talking." Gin snarls at me, "Prime would never—"

Picking a glass up from the table and hurling it at his head effectively cuts off his words. "I'm not fucking Prime! This club isn't run by fucking Prime. He left, stepped down, retired! I am the fucking president here. This is my club. My patch. My family! I run this shit and my word is law! I don't give a fuck if you agree with me or if you don't fucking like my decision, but they're my fucking decisions. I don't have to explain myself to anyone. I speak and you fucking listen. I order and you do. That is the way this fucking world, the Wings of Diablo world, works." I stop to catch my breath and look around the room to see if anyone dares to question me again. "Now, all of you have a choice, you can get your shit ready to go after the Rolling Cobras tomorrow or you can drop your kutte right now. You want to leave get the fuck out, but if you want to be part of this family, it's time for you to realize that Prime's time is over. It's my time now." I look at Max, who has something like pride on his face. "I'm going to get some rest. I want to be on the move by dawn. Make sure we have everything we need." I swing my head to my enforcer, "Wire, I'm going to need your skills. Maybe pack a special bag?"

"Heard." He nods his head without hesitation.

Everyone else just stares at me, but no one has given up their tags yet.

I can feel the tension in the room, and part of me starts to second guess what I'm doing. Maybe I'm wrong. Maybe... no. My mind drifts back to what Laura said. I know what I'm doing. I can lead us to greatness, I just have to stick to what I know is right.

CHAPTER 12

Laura

I SIT ON THE BED, STOCK STILL, AS I LISTEN TO ALEX TRY to defend his position. I knew he was important in the club, but I never took the time to find out who he was. I didn't know he was the president.

My brother was in a race club, which was just a bunch of guys with fast cars. It was absolutely ridiculous to me, but they did have the same sort of dynamic I see here in this clubhouse. There's a president and then those under him. The only difference between my brother's club and this club is Alex is a good man. I may not know him well, but I can feel that down into my soul.

The door to the room opens and Alex hustles in. He slams the door closed behind him, locks it, and leans against it with his eyes closed.

"*Papi*, you okay?" I ask, even though I can see from where I'm sitting that he isn't. He's far from okay.

"No, I'm fucking this up. They don't want me in this position. I'm going to get them killed, maybe they're right." He says, looking up to the ceiling as if he's waiting for the answer to drop down to him, "Maybe I was wrong to think I could handle this. If anything happens to any of them, I don't know what I'd do." He drops his gaze to me, and I see the agony in those expressive eyes. "They're my family. I can't let them down."

I get up from the bed and walk over to him. When I touch him, it's like a live electric wire. I can feel the uncertainty and anguish over this decision ripping his confidence to shreds.

"You won't let them down. You can't Alex. I've been here for an hour tops, and I can see how deep your love is for this club and for them. It's just like when we were trapped in the car. You'd push them all out to safety before you let them hurt, no matter what it means for you. Though I don't know them just from what I know about you, I can bet that most if not all of them are exactly like me. They're not going to leave you, no matter how dangerous or scary things may get. You can lead them. All you have to do is take that first step, and they will follow." I hold his gaze, and he wraps his arms around my waist.

"Laura, where have you been my whole damn life? How the fuck can you make me feel like this so fast?" he tugs me closer to him and doesn't wait for me to answer before he presses his lips to mine. Kissing me so deeply that my knees get weak, and I nearly fall. I don't worry about hitting the ground, though. I trust Alex to catch me with all I am.

It's been less than twenty-four hours that I've known this man, yet I can't see my life without him. He burst into my life, blinding me with the brightness of who he is. I can try to ignore what's happening all I want, but there's no denying that all I recognize is him.

I may not know where this is going, but as long as I can still see him, I know I'll be all right.

CHAPTER 13

Alex

MY EYES POP OPEN A LITTLE BEFORE FIVE IN THE morning, right before dawn. I don't hear anyone moving around yet.

My club is abandoning me before I even get a chance to prove myself. I look over in my bed and see Laura sleeping soundly. Either way, I'm going to make sure she and the rest of my club is safe. These Rolling Cobra motherfuckers are going to figure out just who the fuck they are messing with. I quickly get dressed, even putting on body armor under my shirt and kutte. I grab the guns I do have and put them in my side holsters, one goes in my boot. I have a hunting knife in the other. We don't have much, but I'll use what I have.

I lean down and kiss Laura softly on the forehead, not wanting to wake her up, but her eyes slide open sleepily anyway.

"Make sure you come back to me, *Papi*." She caresses my face and I nod for her. I kiss her again, but this time on her lips. Before we can get too deep into it, a soft tap at my door has me turning around in frustration. Who the hell is knocking on my door at five in the morning?

I walk over and open the door to see Max and Ryder, fully dressed and armed, at my doorway.

"Hey, we're ready to ride." Max says. My eyes slide over to Ryder and though he doesn't say a word, he nods once in my direction.

"Who's we?" I ask and push through the two of them.

Everyone is in the main area looking exactly like Max and Ryder. I didn't think anyone would give up their patch, but I figured at least one or two of them would try to stand down from the fight.

I chuckle when I see Mick pulling the shotgun from behind the bar, "What do you think you doing, old man?"

"Old man? Boy, I may not be able to ride anymore, but I can hold a gun. Let someone come test this old man if they want. It's been a while since I've had to blow someone's head off."

"Well dammit" Clean says, "We blowing heads off? I'm not dressed for that. I got my getting bloody sweatshirt on. I need my exploding brains and gutting motherfuckers one. Gotta look the part, you know."

He smiles at me and I roll my eyes at his ridiculousness.

Wire comes to stand in front of me, all serious, all the time. "What's the plan, Prez? We just running through?" He doesn't ask to be an ass, he genuinely wants to know, so he can be prepared. I look around at everyone waiting for my orders and realize that even if they thought I was doing the wrong thing, there isn't one person here who'd let me do it on my own. The Wings of Diablo is more than just an MC, we're brothers. A bond thicker than the blood we spill and stronger than the metal on our bikes.

I SET EVERYONE UP PERFECTLY. Wire, Gin and Ryder infiltrated the Rolling Cobras clubhouse from the front, while Clean, Max, Larry and I came in from the back. Archer and Mick were both up and away, ready to call out any stragglers or enemies coming up behind us. They were also to make sure that no one got away If I gave the word to kill everyone.

The Rolling Cobras never imagined we'd come straight for them, so when we walk in guns raised, most of them are lounging around with breakfast in their mouth.

"What the fuck, you're dead! Who the fuck do you think you are, strolling in here like you fucking own the place?" Cleve the president of this Rolling Cobra barks at me. He doesn't make a move, though.

"Don't you fucking do it." I hear Max hiss out from beside me and when I look to the side I see one of the assholes that ran me and Laura off the road. He's trying to move away from the confrontation.

My club has the entire Rolling Cobra clubhouse covered. There's nothing any of them can do to get away from what's coming to them.

"This is the fucking club that's been fucking with my livelihood. I'm disappointed. I was sure you'd be ready and armed when we got here. Gunning you down while your people shove fruit loops down their throats takes away from the excitement." I taunt Cleve walking closer to him but keeping his gaze. I don't bother to look around for a threat. If there is one, I know my brothers got my back.

Cleve looks down and sees the president tag on my kutte. "What the fuck is this? You take Prime's place, Alex? I should have known you assholes wouldn't be able to keep up your end of the bargain. Figures, the minute Prime leaves, you try to push your territory over here." Cleve sneers at me, and I'm momentarily stunned.

"What the fuck are you talking about, you went back on the fucking agreement before Prime even left." Ryder spits out before I can recover.

Cleve looks to Ryder then to me, "You got your information mixed up, boy."

I pull my weapon and place it firmly under Cleve's chin. "Call me boy again. I fucking dare you. I don't know what kind of relationship you had with Prime, but I'm not him. You won't disrespect me, and if you continue to do, so I'm going to make sure your club is cleaning your fucking brains off the ceiling from now until Christmas."

Cleve clenches his jaw, but he nods once. I take my gun down but don't put it away, just in case he tries to get out of pocket again.

"I don't have any information mixed up. Your people tried to kill me." I say, and if I wasn't standing right in front of him, I would never have imagined the look on his face. He's confused.

"You attacked first?"

"No, we didn't. You've been burying your drugs on our territory like we wouldn't fucking find it. When we confronted your people, they opened fire on us. Yesterday, four of your guys ran me off the road and into a fucking river. There's no reason for us not to fucking kill you right now." I cross my arms over my chest and wait for his response.

Cleve's a pale skinned Irish man. It's amazing to watch the way his face burns with color. He looks away from me for a second, and I watch as the array of emotions etched on his features turn from confusion to disbelief to rage.

"Who shot at you over the drugs?" He asks me.

"Don't fuck with me, these are your men. You know who you sent." I snap back at him.

"That's the damn problem, I didn't fucking send anyone. As far as I know, the agreement I made with Prime is still intact. If you wouldn't mind pointing out who came for you?" He gestures to his club, and it takes me a second to figure out he's serious.

Instead of walking into a club full of people that want to kill us, we walked into a club full of members that are going against each other.

"Him, that one, this one..." I turn to Wire, "can you remember any others, you were closer."

"That one in the corner, everyone else is dead." He says clearly.

Cleve nods his head, "Vance!" He calls out, and the one in the back slowly moves forward. "Don't fucking make me wait! Get your ass over here!" Cleve yells at the man. He finally gets in front of Cleve and lifts his jaw like he's ready for his punishment.

"Let me have your weapon." Cleve orders, and Vance hands him his gun right away.

I take a step back, thinking that he might turn it on me, but he doesn't. Instead, Cleve continues to talk to Vance.

"You told me that the drop was light because there was an accident. You told me that you got all you could and the rest was lost to us. How is it that you have" He turns to me and asks," How much did you have on your property?"

"A couple kilos." I answer.

Cleve's eyes go wide before he turns back to his patch brother, "How the fuck do you have a couple of kilos to hide anywhere? Did you steal from your brothers? Did you steal from me?"

Vance doesn't say anything.

"Vance, did you skim product from us?" Cleve's voice is calm and even.

"Cleve, I did but I can pay it—" A loud bang echo's through the space, cutting Vance's words off.

I watch in muted shock as Vance blinks a few times and blood dribbles out of the gunshot wound in the center of his head. A second later, he falls straight back and lands with a thud.

"Oh shit." Clean says and stares at the dead man who just fell to the ground.

"You three get the fuck up here," Cleve says, and the

ones I pointed out a moment ago walk slow in our direction. "These the ones that tried to run you off the road?"

"Yeah." I reply.

Cleve nods before turning back to the three of them. "Give me your kuttes."

The three of them argue and fight, giving every excuse they can as to why they shouldn't be removed from the club, but Cleve isn't having it.

"This is my fucking club. I give the damn orders and if you can't abide by them, you don't fucking belong here. You're lucky this man is still fucking alive because if I would've found out that it was because of you assholes that something happened to him, you'd be going the same was as Vance. Now give me your fucking kutte and be grateful I'm not putting a bullet between your eyes." He stares them down and one by one they take their vests off and toss them on the ground.

"Bast, mark these motherfuckers." Cleve calls out and the VP of the Rolling Cobras, Bast walks up with a piece of electronic equipment in his hand. It's red hot. He walks up to each of them, while another of the club holds the men, he presses the red-hot metal to their face and when he pulls back the letter T in a circle is branded fight below their eyes. Finally, he shoots the three of them in their right knee to make sure they can no longer ride. A thorough punishment.

"Alex, Prime was a good president. He knew that peace should be our fucking end goal. Our shit doesn't have anything to do with you and vice versa. I don't want no problems with the Wings. Is this punishment enough to get back on neutral ground?"

I look back to Max, who nods his head. Ryder and Wire do the same.

"Fine, agreed." I put my hand out and Cleve shakes it, I don't release him, "But I think we need to sit down and discuss the changes coming our way. Like you said, Prime was a good president. He's not here anymore. I'm Prez now, and what the Wings of Diablo used to be isn't what we are now."

"I see that." Cleve looks behind me. "I wonder if you'd be more open to an arrangement than your predecessor was. I have a pipeline open on some gun running, but we can't do it as it's a conflict of interest with our drug supplier. It's good money and easy."

"I'm not going to let the guns just float around the town." I answer quickly, if people outside my home-town want to fuck up their community that's on them but not here.

"No, I don't shit where I sleep either. It's over the state lines. You think your boys can handle it?"

I look back at them and I swear I see Ryder bouncing with glee. I look back to Cleve and gesture for Max to come with me

"Let's talk specifics, but I think we can work something out." I clap Cleve's shoulder, and he smiles in return. The crisis is averted. "Wire, tell everyone to stand down. Archer is to stay on watch just in case."

"Heard." Wire says and hustles off to do what I say. The rest of the Wings lower their weapons and start to file out.

"Damn Alex. You wear that patch well. Prime couldn't have picked a better successor. You got more fight in you than half my fucking club put together." Cleve says as he ushers us into a small room with a table.

"It's easy when there's something great to fight for. The Wings of Diablo MC is greater than Prime or me or any of my riders alone. The Wings of Diablo MC is a family and one that I will die to protect. One I will die to see thrive. I'll be a Wing until I die and even then, I'm going to be riding through fucking hell with my patch on my back."

"Shit, talk about fucking inspirational. I can't wait to see this shit play out." Cleve says.

I look down at my kutte and realize this right here is the true start of my Presidency. I can't wait to see how it plays out, either. Bad or good, at least I know it's going to be a wild ride.

<u>THE END</u>

UP NEXT IN THE WINGS OF DIABLO MC

He's the cold-hearted enforcer, she's the angel that saved his life.

I'm the enforcer for the Wings of Diablo MC. Cold and fearless.

The one who shows up in the dark of night with a serrated blade or a piece of barbed wire to bend our enemies to my will.

Nothing gets to me. Nothing until Keeley opens that door to let me in.

Now, one tiny woman holds the key to destroying my entire world. And if I lose her?

Nothing and no one will survive the reign of terror I bring down.

GET YOUR COPY HERE NOW!

MORE FROM RAE B. LAKE

Wings of Diablo MC
Wire
Archer
Clean
Cherry
Prez
Ryder
Ink
Roth
Mack
Storm
Dillon
Pope
Treble

Wings Of Diablo MC - New Orleans

Jameson

Yang

Bones

Pirate

Shyne

Spawns of Chaos MC

Shepard

Tex

Maino

Nitro

Juric Crime Family

Sven's Mark

Josip's Secret

Kaja's Bet

Luka's Captive

Eve's Fury MC

Becoming Vexx

Free

Riot

Duchess

Sugar

Dark Duet

His Darkest Needs

Her Darkest Gift

Boys of Djinn MC
Wyatt
Cody
Spark

Jagged Peaks
Secret Capture
Buried Memories

The Shop Series Books
His Georgia Peach
To Protect and Serve Donut Holes
On The Edge of Ecstasy
His Peach Sparkle

Royal Bastards MC
Death & Paradise
Chaos & Paradise

Standalones
Drunk Love
Saving Valentine

FOLLOW RAE EVERYWHERE!

FACEBOOK

READER GROUP

TWITTER

INSTAGRAM

GOODREADS

AMAZON

WEBSITE

BOOKBUB

NEWSLETTER

TIKTOK